셰익스피어의 그림자

창작극(한영대역)
A play in Korean and English paralleled on the facing pages

셰익스피어의 그림자
Shakespeare's Shadow

송 옥 지음 Written in Korean by Oak Song
문희경 옮김 Translated in English by Hi Kyung Moon

도서출판 동인

지은이의 변

한국셰익스피어학회 창립 60주년을 기념하고자, 극작가도 아닌 한낱 문학도가 처음 써보는 극이라서 흠이 많겠으나, 독자들께서는 너그럽게 받아주셨으면 하는 마음이다.

하나의 극 작품이 완성되려면 플롯, 인물, 주제를 비롯한 소위 '행동의 모방'이라는 연극의 정의에 담긴 요소들이 드러난다. 그러나 이와 같은 아리스토텔레스의 정의에 기반한 전통 서구 드라마의 틀에서 벗어난 <셰익스피어의 그림자>를 대하는 독자/관객은 어리둥절하리라. "이 극을 극이라 할 수 있겠는가? 극이라면, 누구를 위한 극인가?" 이런 의구심이 들 수도 있다. 영문학자이자 영화 평론가인 동료 교수 한 분이 대본을 미리 읽어 본 후, "셰익스피어의 상호텍스트성에 더 밀착한 팩션(fact+fiction)"이라고 했는데, 이는 내가 생각한 셰익스피어의 "그림자" 의미를 그대로 인식하고 반영

한 표현이다. 독자/관객은 그래도 여전히, "그건 그렇다 치고, 밑도 끝도 없는 이 극의 메시지는 도대체 무엇인가?" 이런 질문을 할 여지는 충분히 있다.

셰익스피어의 주인공들 가운데 '악한 주인공(villain heroes)' 이라는 별명이 붙어있는 맥베스와 리처드. 이 두 사람의 대화극 일부를 작년 5월 20일, 한국셰익스피어학회 주관의 '토요 세미나'에서 공연할 기회가 있었다. 그날 참석한 한 친구가 공연장 문을 나서면서 스치는 말로 건넨 한 마디는 내게 선명한 울림으로 와닿았다. "결국 이 두 사람은, 우리도 사람이다, 이 말을 하고 싶은 거구나." 메시지의 답이 무언지 꼭 듣기 원하는 분이 계신다면, 한 친구가 툭 던진 이 말을 그대로 옮겨드리고 싶다.

2인 대화극으로 꾸며진 이 극의 형식을 굳이 따진다면, 일종의 광상극(Extravaganza) 형태로 볼 수 있는 공연 문학(Literature Through the Performance of Duologue for the Reader's Theatre)이라고 할 수 있을지. 엘리자베스 시대에는 연극을 보러 간다기보다는 "들으러 간다"라는 표현을 썼다. TV가 보급되기 전, 한국의 라디오 연속 방송극이 한참 유행하던 50~60년대를 상기해보면, 셰익스피어의 "내 말을 들어 주시오(Lend me your ears!)"라는 대사 그대로, 청취자들은 라디오 앞에 모여 귀를 쫑긋하고 들었다. 이들의 상상력은 눈으로 보는 것 이상의 시계(視界)를 넓힐 수 있었다. 관객 눈에 보이는 게 적으면 적을수록 상상력은 더 활발해진다. “On your imaginary forces work”라는 대사가 말해주듯, 세익스피어는 우리에게 상상력을 요구한다. 그런데 오늘날 관객은 눈에 들어오는 것 이상은 활용하려 하지 않는다. 관객의 창의적 참여가 있을 때 상상력은 더 풍요롭고 강렬해진다. 이것이 암시의 힘이다.

리처드 3세와 맥베스, 그리고 리처드 3세와 오필리아, 이렇게 두 사람씩 쌍을 이루어 나누는 <세익스피어의 그림자>의 각 장면의 대화를 듣는 가운데, 독자/관객께서 사유(思惟)의 유희랄까, 일말의 지적인 운동의 파편을 즐길 수 있다면, 지은이는 이로써 만족한다.

2024년 4월

송 옥

The Author's Preface

This play is written in commemoration of the 60th anniversary of the Shakespeare Association of Korea. Though I have been a student and teacher of literature for many years, I have never written a play before, and therefore ask the reader's indulgence for many of its shortcomings.

The success of a play depends on certain elements, such as plot, character, themes and other ingredients of "mimesis". This play defies all the rules of western drama defined by Aristotle, and may puzzle the audience or readers. How can this be called a play? If a play, for whom is it written? Such questions may well be asked. A colleague of mine, an English literature scholar and critic, read the play as it was in progress and called it "a faction (fact+fiction) that is based on intertextuality of Shakespeare", and I feel this expresses well what I had in mind. But the reader/audience still has the right to ask the question, "What is the message of this rather strange play all about?"

I chose for the play two villain heroes from Shakespeare's many characters. I had an opportunity to perform a part of this duologue in May last year at a seminar hosted by the Association. What one of the audience said in passing as she was leaving left a deep impression on me: "In short I think the two characters, Macbeth and Richard want to say that they too are human, that's what they are trying to say." If anyone is interested to know the answer to what the play is about, these words will partly provide the answer.

The play takes the form of duologue, and perhaps can be considered as a kind of "'Extravaganza' in the form of 'Literature Through the Performance of Duologue for the Reader's Theatre.'" In the Elizabethan era, people went to play not to watch it but to hear it. This reminds of the days before television, the 50s and 60s, when radio broadcasting of dramas was popular in Korea. As in Shakespeare's "Lend me your ears", people would sit all ears before their radios. What they imagined as they listened went beyond what they could see. The less you see with your eyes, the more you imagine. Just as the line "On your imaginary forces work" tells us, Shakespeare demands imagination from us. But today's audience are content merely with what is put before their eyes, and therefore lose the greater riches that can be accrued through more active participation of their imagination. The audience's imagined spectacle can be counted on as more vital, since it arises from the creative participation of each individual. It is the power of suggestion.

If the audience can enjoy something of what might be termed the play of thoughts, a kind of intellectual vortex, while listening to the dialogues of Richard III and Macbeth, of Richard and Ophelia in *Shakespeare's Shadow*, I, as its author, will be content.

April 2024
Oak Song

감사의 글

내가 이 작품을 쓰게 된 계기는 한국셰익스피어학회의 독서/세미나 요청이 있었기 때문이다. 그렇지 않았더라면 이 극은 태어나지 않았을 것이기에 극을 탄생시켜준 학회에 감사한다. 그리고 이 극의 영역을 위해 노고를 아끼지 않으신, 나의 오랜 동료인 고려대학교의 문희경 교수님께 진심으로 감사드린다. 또한 책을 출판해 주신 이성모 사장님과 책의 표지를 맡아주신 이영순 작가님 그리고 이규리 양에게 아울러 충정 어린 감사를 드린다.

Acknowledgements

I would like to give my thanks to the Shakespeare Association of Korea for giving me the idea of writing this play, for had it not been for their request, this play would never have been born. My thanks also goes to Prof. Hi Kyung Moon, a very old colleague of mine at Korea University. I deeply appreciate the great effort she has made in translating the play. I also give my thanks to Mr. Sung-Mo Lee, the publisher, and the artists Youngsoon Lee for the cover design of the book and Gyuri Lee for its image illustration.

| 차례 |

셰익스피어의 그림자

한국셰익스피어학회 60주년 기념을 위한 극

등장인물 리처드 3세, 맥베스, 오필리아
때 2023년 봄날의 어느 맑은 오후
장소 영국 런던의 한적한 공원

Shakespeare's Shadow

Written in commemoration of the 60th anniversary
of the Shakespeare Association of Korea

Dramatis personae Richard III, Macbeth, Ophelia
Time A clear spring afternoon in 2023
Place A quiet park in London

[장면 1] 리처드 3세와 맥베스의 대화.

(페이드인. *리처드는 벤치에 앉아 있고, 맥베스가 그에게 다가온다.*)

리처드 맥베스 형님, 그간 평안하셨는지요?

맥베스 리처드 3세여, 참 오랜만이네. 내가 평안한 때가 언제였는지 기억조차 멍멍하다. 글람즈의 영주 시절이 좋았었지. 그리운 옛날을 돌이켜본들, 무슨 소용 있겠나. 내 모습은 시들은 누런 낙엽에 불과할 뿐. 그다음 발걸음은 어디겠는가? 진정한 종착지— 무덤이지.

리처드 아이고, 형님! 무덤에서 나왔는데, 거기 또 들어가시려고요? 그런 말씀 마시고, 우리 지상에 좀 더 머뭅시다. 때가 되면 난 땅 밑이 아니라, 하늘 위로 가고 싶소.

[Scene 1] Richard III and Macbeth talking.

(Fade in. *Richard is sitting on a bench and Macbeth approaches him.*)

Richard Hello, Macbeth! how are you? Have you been well? At peace, I mean?

Macbeth Richard, my boy! It's been a while since we met. At peace? I can't remember when I was last at peace. Those were the good old days when I was Glamis. But what would be the point of looking back on those dear days? I am no more than "the sere, the yellow leaf" now. And the next step from here? the final destination? — where but the grave.

Richard My dear Macbeth, but you've just come out of the grave. You don't want to go back there. Let's just remain here on earth a little longer. When the time comes, it's not down but up that I want to go.

맥베스 자네가 무슨 수로 하늘나라를 바라보나?

리처드 기도의 힘이지요. 헨리 5세가 아버지 헨리 4세의 범죄를 용서해 달라고, 애진코트 전투에서 홀로 기도하지 않던가요? 선왕 리처드 2세의 왕위를 찬탈하고 부정한 경로로 얻은 아버지의 왕관을 용서해 달라는 아들의 기도는 대견하오. 거룩한 모습이오.

맥베스 아버지 눈 밖에 났던 방탕한 아들 해리가 그렇게 변한 건 놀라워. 불한당들과 밤낮없이 어울리던 망나니 왕자가 명망 높은 헨리 5세로 변하다니. 영국 군사력보다 몇 배나 강한 프랑스를 무찌른 기적의 승리가 애진코트 전투 아닌가?

리처드 헨리 5세는 그 기적의 승리를 하나님의 은혜로, 종교적으로 받아들였소. 군사들은 승전가를 찬송가로 불렀지요. 리처드 2세를 폐위시킨 죄 때문에 불면증에 걸린 헨리 4세도 늘 회개하며 지낸 걸로 알고 있소.

맥베스 헨리 4세는 죄의 사슬에서 벗어나기 위해 예루살렘에서 죽기를 원했다네. 성지에는 못 갔지만, 숨질 때는 '예루살렘'이라고 명명한 궁전의 한 방에서 죽지 않았는가. 하-하.

리처드 그랬지요. 솔직히 형님과 나, 우리 두 사람은 죄인 중의

Macbeth What makes you think that you can even dare to look up to Heaven?

Richard What but the power of prayers. Didn't Henry V pray hard at Agincourt to ask God to forgive his father? There's something becomingly filial about the son begging forgiveness for his father's unjust usurpation of Richard II's throne. There's an air of sublimity about it.

Macbeth Amazing to see that prodigal of a son Harry should have turned out so well, a wastrel who hung out with rogues and ruffians turned into great Henry V, the hero of the miraculous victory of Agincourt, a battle where the English defeated the French army several times more powerful!

Richard Henry thought the battle was won through God's grace and made the army sing *Te Deum*. You know, don't you, that his father the usurper suffered from insomnia and spent the rest of his life in deep repentance?

Macbeth The usurper wanted to expiate his sins by dying in Jerusalem. He didn't make it to Jerusalem though, but made up for it by dying in a room in the palace called Jerusalem, ha ha.

Richard To be frank, both you and I rank as sinners of sinners.

죄인 아니오? 형님은 맥다프의 아내와 그 아이들도 죽였잖소. 나 역시 어린 조카들을 처치했으니, 아동 살해범은 용서받기 어려운 거 아시지요?

맥베스 자네는 나의 가장 뼈아픈 죄악상을 그렇게 지적해야만 하겠나? 여자와 애들을 죽인 건 참 무모한 살인이었네. 그런데, 여보게, 난 살인 얘기는 좀 피하고 싶으이.

리처드 셰익스피어 어른이 써준 독백 중 가장 유명한 건 햄릿의 "사느냐 죽느냐, 그게 문제다." 이거 아니오? 그 한 줄로 온 천지가 뻥 갔소. 『햄릿』 얘기를 모르는 자들도, "사느냐 죽느냐 그게 문제다." 이 한마디는 다 아니까. 그런데, 난 『맥베스』 5막 5장의 형님 독백을 더 빼어나다고 생각하오. "언젠가는 죽어야 할 여인. 언젠가는 그런 말을 들어야 할 때가 올 것이었다. . . . 꺼져라, 꺼져, 단명한 촛불아! 인생은 걸어 다니는 그림자에 불과한 것." 형님한테 궁금한 게 있소. 형수님이 형님께 얼마나 대단한 존재였기에 그런 독백이 나올 수 있었는지, 그게 궁금하오.

맥베스 내 인생이 꼬인 건 바로 그 여자 때문인 건 맞아. 그런데 자넨 지금 와서 왜 그걸 들먹이나? 독백이야 냉소와 유머로 가득 찬 자네의 독백이 일품이지. 막이 오르자마자 들리는 그 첫 마디, "요크 가문의 태양 덕에 이제 불만의 겨울은 가고 영광의 여름을 맞이하게 되었구나." 말더듬이

You killed off Lady Macduff and her children, didn't you? And I, I got rid of my young nephews. As you know, child murder is not easy to forgive.

Macbeth Do you have to point out my worst sin? It was just stupid recklessness to kill women and children. Look here, Richard, I really don't want to talk about murder.

Richard You know the most famous line by great Shakespeare is Hamlet's "To be or not to be, that is the question". That single line captivated the whole world. Even people who don't know the play have heard of it. But in my opinion, your soliloquy in Act 5 is better: "She should have died hereafter: There would have been a time for such a word– . . . out, out, brief candle! Life's but a walking shadow". I'm curious what Lady Macbeth had in her to inspire such lines from you.

Macbeth My dear Richard, my life became a mess because of her. But why mention that now. As far as soliloquies are concerned, yours equals none, so full of humour and cynicism it is. As soon as the curtain rises, those superb first lines: "Now is the winter of our discontent/ Made glorious summer by this sun of York". George VI used these words to treat his

조지 6세가 언어 치료로 사용했던 대사 아닌가. 오죽하면 자네의 그 "불만의 겨울"을 존 스타인벡이 소설 제목으로 썼겠나?

리처드 아, 그렇게 치자면, 형님의 열두 줄짜리 독백이야말로, 프로스트에게 "꺼져라, 꺼져!" 시 제목도 제공했고, 포크너의 소설 『음향과 분노』도 거기서 나오지 않았습니까? 형님, 셰익스피어 문구를 누가 이용했나, 그런 건 관심 없고요. 내가 알고 싶은 건, 형님이 애처가냐 공처가냐? 어느 쪽이었는지 그게 알고 싶소. 나나 형님이나 악한 주인공으로 유명하지만, 나야 원래 그런 놈이라 치고, 사려 깊고 우아한 맥베스 장군께서는 어쩌다 그런 악명의 주인공이 된 거요?

맥베스 성경 말씀대로, 욕심이 잉태한즉 죄를 짓고 사망을 낳은 거지. 아담은 하나님과의 언약을 어기고 이브 핑계를 댔지만, 난 내 아내 탓이라고만 할 수 없네.

리처드 마녀들 꼬임에 걸려든 거지요.

맥베스 마녀들 꼬임? 마녀들이 내가 왕이 되는 상상을 내 머릿속에 불어 넣은 건 맞아. 그렇지 않고서야 왜 내 눈앞에 단도가 뱅뱅거렸겠나? 그런 환상의 칼을 내가 왜 잡으려고 애썼겠냐고. 내 머릿속에는 덩컨 왕을 죽이고 싶은 욕망이 강렬했던 거지. 왕을 죽인 나는 저주받고 불면증에 시달렸어.

stammer, did you know? No wonder John Steinbeck took up that fine expression "the winter of our discontent" for the title of his novel.

Richard If we are to talk of such things, your twelve-line soliloquy gave Frost the poem "Out, out—", not to mention Faulkner's *Sound and Fury*. But Macbeth, I'm not interested in who took what from Shakespeare. What I really want to know is whether you were a devoted husband or merely a henpecked one. I want to know which. Both you and I are notorious villains, and I admit that I am such a one, but what made you into a villain, so serious and valiant a general that you were?

Macbeth As the Bible says, evil desire engendered sin and death. Adam broke his pledge to God and laid the blame on Eve, but as for me, I can't say it was my wife's fault.

Richard Then the witches, they tricked you?

Macbeth The witches? Nah! It's true that they put the idea of becoming king into my head. Otherwise, how can you explain the dagger dancing before my eyes and my trying to grab it? There was already in my head a strong desire to kill Duncan. I was cursed for killing the king and suffered from terrible insomnia

나도 헨리 4세처럼 잠을 죽였어.

리처드 그런데 말이오, 형님처럼 인내심 강하고, 치밀한 분이 왕관을 쓰기가 무섭게 흉악한 길로 치달았다는 사실이 놀랍소. 형님은 능력 있고, 냉정하리만큼 철저한 분이오. 나이는 지긋해도 겉모습은 여전히 몸짱에 얼짱에, 악기도 잘 다루는 멋쟁이 노신사. 부럽소! 사람들이 기피하는 나 리처드와는 천지 차이요. 사람 모가지 치는 재주밖에 없는 찌그러진 절뚝발이 리처드와는 정반대의 인물이 형님이잖소.

맥베스 리처드, 자네에게는 나름의 특유한 매력이 있네. 자기가 꾸민 끔찍한 죄상을 유머러스하게 말하는 비상한 재주. 냉소적인 독특한 유머, 그거 아무나 할 수 있는 거 아니네. 자네의 언술은 관객을 사로잡는다니까. 앤 부인 말이야. 자네가 그녀의 남편 에드워드 왕세자를 튜크스베리 전투에서 죽이고 그녀의 시아버지 헨리 6세를 죽인 장본인 아닌가? 자네에게 온갖 독설을 퍼붓던 왕세자비를 무슨 수로 단숨에 홀렸나? 그것도 시아버지 장례식 행렬에서 말일세.

in consequence. Like Henry IV, I murdered sleep.

Richard But I'm surprised that a man so steady and thorough as you could choose such an evil path the moment the crown was on your head. You are a man of great ability, level-headed and prudent. Considering your age, you look fit and are still handsome enough, and a great musician too, altogether a fine old gentleman. I envy you. So different from me whom everyone despises and avoids. You are the very opposite of a limping cripple like me, who am good at nothing but chopping off heads.

Macbeth Richard dear boy, you have your own talents and charms. Not everyone is capable of your extraordinary ability to describe terrible deeds in humorous terms, nor of your peculiar brand of cynical humour. The words from your mouth have power to hold the audience, I assure you. Well, just consider the case of Lady Anne. You killed her husband Edward, Prince of Wales, in the battle of Tewkesbury, and her father-in-law Henry VI too. She used to heap venomous words on your head. But how you managed to charm her completely, and at her father-in-law's funeral too, I'm just lost for words.

리처드 여자들은 대체로 감상적이라오. 당신에 대한 사랑이 그 원인이었다, 당신을 얻기 위해서였다, 이렇게 말하면, 여자 마음 절반은 이미 얻은 거요. "그대의 아름다움이 살육의 원인이었소. 꿈속에서도 그대의 고혹적인 아름다움이 날 미치게 사로잡았소. 세상 남자들을 다 처치해서라도 그대의 품에 한 시간만이라도 안길 수만 있다면!" 이렇게 호소하고, 그러고는 날 죽이라고 그녀 손에 칼을 들려줍니다. 무릎 꿇고, 맨가슴을 들이대는 거요. 찌르라고요. 여자들은 강렬한 말과 제스처에 녹아요.

맥베스 그럼 앤 부인이 자네의 능청에 속은 거야?

리처드 그건 내가 그녀를 속인 게 아니라, 그 여자가 어리석고 가볍다 보니 스스로 속은 거요.

맥베스 그녀를 사랑한 건 전혀 아니었다, 그 말이지?

리처드 사랑은 무슨! 난 오직 대권을 잡으려고 킹메이커 노릇 하던 그녀 아버지 워릭 백작의 힘이 필요했을 뿐이오. 앤을 취하자마자 즉시 없앨 궁리부터 했으니까. 난 형님과는 달라요. 형님은 살인자가 아니오. 타고난 범죄자가 아니라고요. 어쩌다 발 한번 잘못 딛고 그렇게 된 거 아니겠소?

맥베스 순간의 선택이 운명을 좌우한다! 내가 그 꼴이 난 건 사실이네.

리처드 난 갈등이 없소. 해치워야 한다면 그 즉시 그걸로 끝이오.

Richard Well, women are generally susceptible. When you whisper words like "I did it because of my love for you, to gain you", then you're half way to success. "Your beauty was the cause of that effect;/ Your beauty, that did haunt me in my sleep/ To undertake the death of all the world,/ So might I live one hour in your sweet bosom." Utter such words and present her a dagger. Kneel and bare your breast, and tell her to stab you. Women find strong words and gestures irresistible, you know.

Macbeth So Anne was completely taken in by your guile, eh?

Richard I didn't deceive her, she deceived herself because she was foolish and thoughtless.

Macbeth Do you mean you had no love for her at all?

Richard Love? Look here, I merely needed her to get her father, kingmaker Warwick's support. The moment I won her, I was busy thinking of ways of popping her off. I'm not like you. You're not a murderer, not a born criminal, if you know what I mean. You took a wrong step somewhere and ended up being one, wouldn't you agree?

Macbeth You're right. I made a single bad choice and my fate was sealed.

Richard I don't suffer from qualms. If I have to do it, I do

오죽하면 『리처드 3세』 연극 광고를, "그자의 목을 쳐라!" "왕국을 줄 테니 말 한 필을 다오!" 이런 해괴한 광고판을 내걸겠소? 나도 보즈워스 전투에서 열심히 싸웠소. 그러던 중, 말 한 필 부르짖다 리치먼드의 칼에 맞아 죽었소. 그때 장면을 떠올리면 쪽팔려요.

맥베스 그런데 난데없이 나라와 말 한 필을 바꾸겠다는 발상은 어디서 나온 게야?

리처드 내가 타던 백마가 죽으니 맨땅에서 싸우게 되었답니다. 투구도 잃었고요. 리치먼드, 그자가 머리를 썼더라고. 리치먼드로 알고 내가 죽인 놈이 다섯이나 되었는데, 모두 가짜였소. 말을 잃고 궁지에 몰린 절박한 상황에서, 일단 목숨부터 건지고 보자. 그래야 싸울 것 아니냐? 배고파 죽겠다고, 팥죽 한 그릇에 장자권 팔아넘긴 에서보다야 낫지 않소?

맥베스 아무튼 자네는 비상해. 중상모략, 위장술, 임기응변, 다 자네의 전매품 아닌가. 왕위를 빼앗기 위해서 자신만만하게 음모를 예언하고, 신속하게 이를 실천하는 악의 천재라고나 할까?

it and that's the end of it. Look at the awful lines they put in the posters for my play. "Off with his head!" "A horse, a horse! my kingdom for a horse!" I really fought hard at Bosworth, you know. It just happened that I was yelling for a horse in the thick of the battle when I got struck down by Richmond. When I think of that moment, I'm ashamed.

Macbeth Where did you get that strange idea of exchanging your kingdom for a horse?

Richard Well, it happened like this. My horse fell and I was on the ground fighting. I had lost my helmet too. Richmond, oh he was clever! I thought I had killed him when another Richmond would appear. I killed five Richmonds, you know. By that time I was desperate, and my first thought was to save my neck, for how could I go on fighting without a neck? Isn't mine a better case than Esau's who sold the eldest son's rights for a bowl of red pottage merely because he was hungry?

Macbeth You are a great man, at any rate. Slander, camouflage, improvisation, you're a master of these. You plotted to take the crown and went about it with no loss of time. It's the work of a, let's say, a genius, a genius of evil.

리처드 그런데 말이오. 참 이상하오. 왕관을 차지한 3막 후반부터는 내가 이전처럼 악행을 즐기지 못하겠더라고요. 내가 무슨 짓을 한 거냐? 이런 짐 덩어리 쇠고랑을 머리에 얹으려고? 옥좌라는 이름의 가시방석에 앉으려고? 그러려고 기를 쓰고 악행을 저질렀단 말이냐? 우리 어머니가 나를 가리켜 "잔혹한 위인"이라고 불렀소.

맥베스 리처드 3세의 참회록이라도 쓰고 싶은 건가?

리처드 자괴감에 허탈했지요. 형수님 생각이 납디다. 맥베스 부인도 왕비가 된 3막 이후부터는 완전히 힘을 잃고 혼이 나갔잖소. 난 허무감에 빠졌지, 혼이 빠지진 않았소만. 형님, 그런데 말이오. 내 이름이 악인으로 형님과 나란히 세상 입에 오르는 걸 난 괘념치 않소. 그렇지만 셰익스피어의 가장 악명 높은 인물로 이아고와 나를 비교하던데, 그건 정말 불쾌하오. 그런 족보도 없는 무식한 양아치와 왕족인 나를 비교하다니! 자존심 상합니다. 이아고 대사 중에 멋진 게 한 줄이라도 있으면 대보시오. 없어요, 없어! 머리통에 든 건 질시와 악뿐인 야만인! 오셀로 역을 햄릿이 맡았

Richard But you know what? A most strange thing happened. After I got the crown, I found I couldn't enjoy villainy as before. Thoughts like, "What have I done? All for a burdensome piece of iron on my head? To sit on a seat of thorns? Was it worth it to have strained everything in me for it?" Thoughts like these would occur to me. My mother once called me "a bloody man", you know.

Macbeth You're not thinking of writing a confession surely?

Richard I was full of self-doubt and my self-esteem suffered, I assure you. That reminds me of Lady Macbeth. After she became queen in the third act, she completely lost her strength and her mind too. As for me, I was dejected enough, though I didn't go as far as to lose my mind. But to change the subject, I have no objection to my name being coupled with yours as the two worst villains in Shakespeare. But people often compare me with Iago, and to that I strongly object. How dare they compare me, a royal, with that low-born vulgar rogue. My pride won't suffer it. Tell me if you can find one single good line he utters. Absolutely none. He's a rogue with nothing in his head but envy and venom. It's Hamlet who should have played Othello. Iago would

어야 했는데. 그러면 그 녀석은 햄릿을 속이려다 3막도 끝나기 전에 햄릿 칼에 쓰러지든지, 아니면 철창신세가 될 게 뻔하지.

맥베스 이보게, 그건 안되지. 그렇게 되면 극의 줄거리도 없어지고, 시작도 끝도 없으면, <오셀로 비극>은 성립할 수 없지.

리처드 난 이런 상상을 해봅니다. 햄릿이 클레오파트라를 만났어도 안토니처럼 "창녀의 노리개" 소리를 들었을까? 절세의 미녀가 유혹하는데 마다할 위인은 없겠지. . . . 과연 노골적인 성적 유혹에 햄릿이 넘어갈까? 필경 얼마간 재미 보다가, 여인의 손아귀에서 빠져나갈 게 뻔합니다.

맥베스 자네가 극을 하나 써보는 게 어때?

리처드 극을 아무나 쓰나요? 내가 책 읽는 건 좋아하오. 그러나 펜 잡이는 아니오. 난 칼잡이라오. 그놈 이아고가 유명한 이유를 모르겠단 말이야.

맥베스 이보게, 자네 이아고를 얕보는 경향이 있는데, 결코 머리 나쁜 자가 아닐세. 어쩌다 그에게 꽂혔나? 이아고 유령이라도 본 게야?

리처드 유령 얘기는 제발 하지 마시오! 나 때문에 희생된 자들의 혼령이 꿈에 줄줄이 나타납니다. 그것만도 식은땀 나는데! 형님은 방쿼 유령 하나만 보고도 기절초풍했잖소.

have tried his tricks on Hamlet, and before the third act was over, Hamlet would have done him in with his sword or had him thrown into prison.

Macbeth My dear boy, that won't do. That would ruin the whole story. There would be no head or tail to it and would spell the end of "The Tragedy of Othello".

Richard Speaking of Hamlet, I sometimes imagine a situation like this. If Hamlet had met Cleopatra, would he have ended up being called "a strumpet's fool"? No man can withstand the allures of such a beauty, I admit, but would he have been seduced by her charms, I wonder? I think not. He would have fooled around a bit and slipped away.

Macbeth Why not try your hand at writing a play yourself?

Richard No, I love reading but I'm not a scribbler. I am a swordsman. But going back to Iago, it beats me why he should be so famous.

Macbeth You look down on Iago but he's not stupid, you know. Why are you harping on about him? Have you come across his ghost or something?

Richard Please don't talk of ghosts. I'm bothered by a host of them all night in my dreams. They have me in a sweat. You saw only one, Banquo's, and you were a wreck.

맥베스 앤 부인 말로는 자네도 잠 못 이루는 밤이 많았다고 하던데. 혼령 모가지는 댕강 자르지 못하겠던가?

리처드 형님도, 참! 혼령은 환영이오. 그림자를 내가 어쩌겠소? 형님, 내가 정말 꿈에 볼까 두려운 자들이 누군지 아시오? 리어왕의 그 악하고 독한 딸년들이라오. 고너릴과 리건! 이 계집들은 사랑이 무언지를 모르오. 사랑과 애욕의 차이도 구별 못 하는 천박한 종자들! 같은 부모한테 태어난 고상한 코딜리어와는 어찌 그리 다를꼬?

맥베스 자넨, 사돈 남 말하듯 하네. 어쨌든 인류 최초의 살인은 가인이 아벨을 죽인 형제간의 살인이었다는 것을 기억하게.

리처드 가인은 아벨을 왜 죽인 거요? 뺏고 빼앗길 옥좌도 없었는데.

맥베스 질투심이지.

리처드 온 인류에 타락을 가져온 한 사람이 있었다. 그런데 지금부터 이천여 년 전에, 타락한 온 인류를 구하기 위해 또 한 사람이 태어났다. 그런데 그 두 사람 모두 같은 조물주의 손으로 창조되었다. 멋지지 않소? 결자해지가 아니겠소?

맥베스 리처드, 자넨 엉뚱한 생각도 잘하는군.

리처드 시작은 이미 인류 첫 자식부터 그랬으니, 내 차례까지 기다릴 것도 없었군. 나야말로 왕관을 차지하려고 걸림돌을

Macbeth Lady Anne once told me you spent sleepless nights because of them. Weren't you able to chop off their heads?

Richard Come on, Macbeth. Ghosts are illusions, shadows. I can't touch them. Do you know who I'm really afraid to see in my dreams? Lear's demonic daughters, Goneril and Regan! Their malicious nature gives them no understanding of what love is. They can't tell love from lust. It's hard to believe they're of the same stock as Cordelia.

Macbeth You talk as if the same doesn't apply to us all. Don't forget that man's first murder was a fratricide.

Richard I want to know why Cain killed Abel, when there was no crown at stake.

Macbeth Mere envy, I should say.

Richard Listen. Through one man the entire race of men fell. Another man was born two thousand years ago to save them. Both come from the same Creator. Don't you find that neat? You have to pay for your deeds, you know. There's no avoiding it.

Macbeth You do have odd ideas in your head, Richard.

Richard The first born of man was a murderer and so am I one. I got rid of all the obstacles on my way to the

모조리 제거했으니까. 악한 리처드 글로스터! 그게 소문난 내 프로필이라니!

맥베스 일을 저지르고 나서 후회해본들 무슨 소용 있겠나?

리처드 그런데 형님, 내 마음속 깊이 맴도는 풀리지 않는 숙제가 하나 있소.

맥베스 그게 뭔데?

리처드 나, 나쁜 놈 맞아요. 그렇지만, 내가 과연 셰익스피어가 써준 대로 그렇게까지 포악한 자였을까요? 그게 사실이라면 나는 골백번, 아니, 골 천 번 죽어 마땅하오. 난 내가 왕이 되려는 야심으로 독하게 행동했고, 나의 영광을 사랑한 죄, 인정하오. 그러나 내게도 형수님이 말하는 "어려운 사람에 대한 동정심" 그런 따듯한 구석이 있답니다. 리처드가 과연 셰익스피어가 써준 모습 그대로, 그렇게까지 포악하기만 했을까, 의구심이 듭니다.

맥베스 자네가 악한 짓 한 건 사실 아닌가? 여보게, 우리 추한 얘기 그만하고, 관심을 다른 데로 돌려보는 게 어때? 햄릿에 관한 얘기 좀 해보세. 햄릿의 복수 지연에 대한 설은 무성하지만, 내게는 여전히 풀리지 않는 수수께끼거든. 자네 생각이 어떤지, 좀 들려주게.

리처드 그거 햄릿 성격이 복잡해서 꼬여 보일 뿐이오. 시대적 관점

throne, so I go down in history as Richard of Gloucester the Villain. That's my name, I regret to say.

Macbeth What would be the point of having regrets after the deed is done?

Richard But dear Macbeth, there's a nagging doubt I can't get rid of.

Macbeth What would that be?

Richard I admit I am a villain. But am I the devil Shakespeare made me out to be? If I am, I deserve death a thousand times over. I had an ambition to become king and did evil and gloried in it. I admit it. But a devil that I am, there's within me a warm spot somewhere, the milk of human kindness as your wife would put it. So I have doubts about my being as infamous as Shakespeare had me painted.

Macbeth Come, come, you know what you've done. Let's dwell no more on such unpleasant things and talk about something else. Let's talk about Hamlet. There are so many theories on why he procrastinated over his revenge, but it still has me in the puzzle. What are your views?

Richard Hamlet himself is a difficult case, that's why the whole thing looks complicated. It's simple if you look at it from the perspective of the age he lived in.

에서 보면 간단하오. 햄릿이 유학한 곳이 어디요?

맥베스 위텐버그 대학 말인가?

리처드 위텐버그가 어떤 대학입니까? 종교 개혁을 일으킨 마틴 루터 학교 아닙니까? 말하자면, 햄릿은 철저한 르네상스 인간이오. 다시 말해서 햄릿은 아버지가 속한 중세 사회와 그가 속한 변화하는 현대 문화, 그 사이에 끼어 번민하는 청년이었소.

맥베스 그건 이해가 되네. 르네상스는 역사의 획을 긋는, 오늘날 현대로 이어지는 전혀 다른 시대니까. 그래도 복수해 달라는 아버지 유령의 뜻을 따르려고 애는 썼지. 극중극까지 꾸며서 유령의 정체와 클로디어스의 범죄 사실도 증명했겠다.

리처드 그런데, 그것도 잠깐이오. "원수 갚는 일은 하나님 소관이니, 너는 가만있거라." 이러지도 저러지도 못하는 딱한 청년. 그렇지만, 이 청년은 어차피 골 빠지게 생각만 할 뿐, 실행은 말짱 꽝이라오. 노르웨이 왕자 포틴브라스가 덴마크 땅을 통과하면서 폴란드 전쟁 출정식을 했잖소. 이를 지켜보고 내린 햄릿의 결론을 기억하시오? "아, 이제부터는 나도 생각을 독하게 갖자. 그렇지 않으면 난 천하에 가치 없는 놈이다!" 이자의 말인즉, 행동을 독하게 하는 게 아니라, 생각을 독하게 갖자는 거 아니오? 생각을 수백 번 독하

Where did Hamlet study?

Macbeth You mean Wittenberg?

Richard And what kind of place is Wittenberg? Isn't it the same university where Luther had studied, the cradle of Reformation? In a word, in Hamlet you see a perfect Renaissance man. He was a youth torn between his father's medieval world and the changing modern world he belonged to.

Macbeth That makes sense. The Renaissance was a watershed that ushered in an entirely new era. He tried hard, though, to keep his ghostly father's wish for revenge. He even staged a play-within-a play to expose Claudius.

Richard But that's the sum total of what he did. But then, we're not supposed to do anything. "'Vengeance is mine, and I will repay', says the Lord." He was caught in-between and could do nothing, poor lad. But then, he was always buried in deep thoughts and was no good at taking any action. Do you remember what Hamlet said when he saw Norway's Fortinbras cross over to Danish soil on his way to fight Poland? "Let my thoughts be bloody, or be nothing worth." What he meant was bloody in thoughts only and no action. What's the use of having a thousand thoughts

게 먹은들, 행동이 따르지 않으면 무슨 소용 있겠소? 그러니, 그 많은 독백을 읊으면서 혼자 헤매고 다니는 거라오.

맥베스 자네 혹시 셰익스피어가 마음에 안 드나? 햄릿이 마땅치 않은가?

리처드 형님 질문의 요지가 뭐요?

맥베스 글쎄, 자네 언어가 좀 비딱하게 들려서 그러네. 셰익스피어가 위대한 작가라고 생각지 않나?

리처드 무슨 자다 봉창 뚫는 소리요? 저 꼭대기 왕족에서부터 귀족, 평민, 그리고 밑바닥 날품팔이에 이르기까지, 아니 저 악명 높은 노상강도 가말리엘 랫시조차 열광한 작가요. 그 당시 케임브리지 학자 가브리엘 하비도 셰익스피어는 분별력 없는 관객이나 식견 높은 관객이나 할 것 없이, 두루두루 만족시킨다고 했소. 그 유명한 에밀리 디킨슨이 셰익스피어 전집을 다 읽고 나서, 뭐라고 했는지 아시오? 조신하고 음전한 이 19세기 미국 여성의 입에서 터진 탄성이오. "이제 세상에 무슨 책이 더 필요하리오?" 맥베스 형님, 내가 여기 대고 무슨 말을 하리오? 셰익스피어 등장 이후, 오늘날까지 전 세계의 변함없는 베스트셀러 두 권, 성경과 셰익스피어. 이게 무얼 말해줍니까? 그런데 말입니다. 셰익스피어와 동갑내기인 크리스토퍼 말로 있잖소? 난 이 친구한테 관심이 있소. 그가 스물아홉 나이에 요절하지 않았

if you can't act on them? That's why he wanders about soliloquizing endlessly.

Macbeth Dear boy, don't you like Shakespeare? Don't you approve of Hamlet?

Richard What do you mean?

Macbeth I mean, you sound a bit critical. Don't you think that Shakespeare is a great man?

Richard Of course I think so! From the royals at the very top down to the commoners and to the lowest drudges, even to that notorious highway robber Gamaliel Ratsey, they couldn't praise him enough. You know, a contemporary of his, Cambridge scholar Gabriel Harvey, said Shakespeare was for everyone, the ignorant and the learned likewise. Do you know what Emily Dickinson, that quiet lady-like 19th-century American poet, said after she had completed her readings of Shakespeare? "Why is there any other book needed?" What can I add to this statement? There are two unvarying best-sellers in the world, Shakespeare and the Bible. What does that tell you about him? Shakespeare had a contemporary, Christopher Marlowe. You know him? As a matter of fact, I find Marlowe somewhat interesting. If he hadn't been cut off at twenty-nine,

더라면 셰익스피어를 능가했을지도 몰라요. 이건 어디까지나 나의 가정법이니까, 토는 달지 마시고.

맥베스 크리스토퍼 말로! 그 이름, 내가 좋아하는 멋진 이름이지! 내게 아들이 있다면 그와 똑같은 이름을 지어주고 싶다네.

리처드 와! 형님, 인간미가 철철 넘칩니다그려! 맥베스의 아들, 크리스토퍼 말로 맥베스! 눈물 나려 하오.

맥베스 그런데, 자네 생각에는 그가 그렇게까지 대단한가? 처음으로 무운 시를 구사한 공로가 있지.

리처드 파우스트 박사의 대사 한 줄이 나를 기절시켰다오.

맥베스 어느 한 줄이 그대를 쓰러트렸는고?

리처드 "트로이 대신에 위텐버그가 파괴되라!" 눈부신 이 한 줄이 내 뒤통수를 때렸소. 좀 전에 형님이 르네상스는 역사의 획을 긋는 중요한 시대라고 했잖소? 햄릿의 두통을 앓게 한, 지적 윤리적 갈등의 시대 말이오.

맥베스 르네상스는 고대 그리스 문화와 기독교 문화, 윤리 개념이 서로 다른 두 개의 문화를 융합하려 했으니, 갈등이 많고, 당연히 불안정할 수밖에. 그런 까닭에 비극 장르가 가장 왕성했던 시대이기도 하지.

리처드 헬레니즘과 기독교 문화의 통합? 그리스 고전 사상과 기독교 사상의 융합? 그게 가능키나 한 얘기요? 어불성설이오. 기독교 인문주의? 듣기에는 참으로 그럴듯합니다. 구수하게

he might have surpassed Shakespeare. This is just a supposition, so don't start arguing.

Macbeth Christopher Marlowe! That's a name I like, a beautiful name. If I had a son, I would name him after Marlowe.

Richard You're full of human kindness today. Macbeth's son, Christopher Marlowe Macbeth! I find that rather moving.

Macbeth Do you really think there is greatness in Marlowe? He did invent blank verse, I suppose.

Richard A line from *Dr. Faustus* had me stunned.

Macbeth Which line?

Richard "Instead of Troy shall Wittenberg be sacked." This brilliant line took my breath away. You told me the Renaissance was a watershed, a period of moral and intellectual conflicts that gave Hamlet such headaches.

Macbeth The Renaissance tried to fuse ancient cultures with Christianity, cultures with different moral values, and that naturally caused conflicts and instabilities. That's why tragedies thrived in that period, you know.

Richard Fuse Hellenism with Christianity, a synthesis of classicism and Christianity? Is that possible? Christian Humanism – it's a far-fetched idea. Though I must admit it has a good ring to it. But a mongrel word

들립니다. 그러나 기독교 인문주의라는 합성어 같은 이 단어는 로미오가 말하는 "차가운 불" "병든 건강"—이처럼 모순어법, 쇠똥 빠진 소리요. 아킬레스와 예수, 서로 어울리기나 하오? 오만하고 복수심 강한 고대 그리스의 영웅 아킬레스와 오른쪽 뺨을 치거든 왼쪽 뺨도 내주라는 용서와 겸손의 기독교의 영웅, 예수 그리스도. 지향하는 문명의 미덕이 이렇게 서로 반대로 어긋난 두 사람이 어울리기나 하냐고요.

맥베스 자네 말은 틀리지 않네. 르네상스를 영국에 들여온 에라스무스도 그 점을 우려했으니까. "그리스도와 연합한 너희가 어찌 알렉산더 대왕의 길로 슬그머니 돌아가려 하느냐?" 경고했지. 이교도를 기독교화하는 게 아니라, 기독교를 이교도화하는 결과를 두려워했기 때문에 종교 개혁자들도 좋아하진 않았네.

리처드 기독교의 창조 질서는 인간의 생명을 중시하고 가치와 존엄을 기초로 하고 있지 않소. 인문주의 사고와 통하는 부분이 있지요. 그래서 당시 작가들이 이 두 개념을 부드럽게 녹여보려고 시도했는데, 핵심을 인식하지 못했던 거요. 파우스트 박사는 마법의 힘으로 문자 그대로 아득한 그리스를 되살리려 했소. "트로이 대신에 위텐버그가 파괴되라!" 루터의 도시를 헥터의 도시로 대신할 것을 바란다는 이 한마디는 르네상스 주제를 퍽 찌른 거요.

like Christian Humanism is, like Romeo's icy fire or sick health, an oxymoron, mere quibble. Put Achilles and Jesus in the same melting pot and see how that works. Achilles, the proud and vengeful Greek hero, and Jesus the Christian hero who preaches humility and forgiveness, who tells you to present the left cheek if someone should slap your right. Is there any chance that these two who pursue such widely different virtues will get along?

Macbeth You have a point there. Erasmus was troubled by that too. So he warned: "You have allied yourself with Christ – and yet will you slide back into the ways of Alexander the Great?" They were afraid that they would end up paganizing Christians, not the other way round and that put the reformers off.

Richard Respect for human life and human dignity is a value Christianity is based on, and this is what it shares with Humanism. So writers tried to merge the two cultures, but they failed to get to the heart of the problem. Faustus tried to revive ancient Greece through magic: "Instead of Troy shall Wittenberg be sacked"! He was trying to replace the city of Hector with the city of Luther. He touched the very nub of the Renaissance.

맥베스 육체적 미를 추구하는 건 고대 그리스와 로마인들에게는 미덕이지만, 기독교에서는 이를 죄로 간주한다. 그러므로 트로이의 헬렌은 이교도의 완벽한 미녀지만, 기독교 관점에서 보면 파우스트 박사를 육체적 음욕의 파멸로 이끈 마녀다. 이 말인가?

리처드 바로 그거요. 형님이 정곡을 찔러 주었소. 그리스 고전의 미가 르네상스 현대에서 죄로 나타난 거지요.

맥베스 하기야 영적 문제는 차원이 다른 얘기지. 존경받는 위텐버그 최고의 학자, 최고의 과학자, 최고의 스승. 그런 지성인이 그렇게 무너질 수 있다는 게 놀라워.

리처드 욕망, 욕심. 형님도 욕심이 잉태한즉 사망을 낳았다고 했잖소.

맥베스 파우스트 같은 위대한 학자가 지상 최대의 지식에 만족하지 못하고, 마법을 원하다니! 신적 존재가 되려는 욕망에 사로잡히다니!

리처드 마법으로 신이 되기를 원한다? 그건 상상할 수도 없는 일이오. 참, 바라는 은사도 가지가지요!

맥베스 파우스트 박사는 비범한 인물임에는 틀림이 없어.

리처드 파우스트의 신령 놀이는 끝났소! 피로 맺은 24년, 계약 만료! 지옥을 알리는 최후의 종소리! 땡! 고대 그리스/로마의 가치와 기독교 가치의 갈등이 어떻게 비극의 토대를 제공

Macbeth Pursuing physical beauty is a virtue to the ancients but a sin to Christians. From a pagan point of view, Helen of Troy is the perfection of beauty. From a Christian one, she's a witch who led Faustus into lust and destruction. Might that be your meaning?

Richard You hit the nail on the head. Beauty in the ancient world, Sin in these modern days.

Macbeth The foremost, the most respected scholar of Wittenberg, its greatest scientist, teacher, and intellectual, how could such a man fall to pieces in such a way? It doesn't bear thinking about.

Richard Lust for power, ambition, greed, whatever. Didn't you say that evil desire engendered death?

Macbeth To think that such a great scholar like Faustus shouldn't content himself with earthly knowledge but covet magic to deify himself.

Richard Become a god through magic? Sheer madness! There was no end to his ambition, it seems.

Macbeth But for all that, he has some greatness.

Richard His days of playing god are over. The contract, signed with blood, lasted only twenty-four years. The term expires, the bell tolls, the jaws of hell gape. Do you know what Marlowe showed? He showed how the clash of ancient cultures with Christianity laid

했느냐? 그걸 말로가 보여 주었소. 그런 점에서 존 밀턴 선생께서는 『실낙원』의 공식을 암시해 준 공로자 말로에게 고맙다고 해야 할 것이오.

맥베스 최후의 순간에는 파우스트가 회개하고 허우적댔지만 소용없었지. 고대 세계의 부, 재물, 미, 지혜, 권력, 이 모든 걸 탐냈던 파우스트. 추락한 울지 추기경의 자조 섞인 탄식이 들리네. "세상의 허망한 부귀영화여, 네가 증오스럽구나. 그래서 넘어지면 루시퍼가 넘어지듯, 두 번 다시 일어날 희망조차 없는 것을." 인류의 타락을 가져온 최초의 인간, 아담의 길을 파우스트가 그대로 따라간 거야. 사실 우리가 어두운 비극 세계에서 느끼는 감동은 극한의 고통을 인간의 힘으로 승화시키는 시적인 변화에 있거든.

리처드 시적인 변화요? 형님! 그런 건 평론가들이 즐기는 문학적 수사에 불과하오. 현실성 없는 헛소리요.

맥베스 여보게, 그게 무슨 망발인가? 독자의 길잡이인 문학 비평을 그렇게 뭉개버리면 쓰나? 말이 왜 그리 삐딱해? 어느 때 보면 자넨 청개구리 같아.

리처드 평론가들이 떠벌리는 고답적 수사가 마땅치 않을 뿐이오.

맥베스 자네 참 맹랑하군. 평론가들은 생각과 의식을 깨우쳐주는

grounds for tragedy. From that perspective, John Milton should thank Marlowe for showing him the formula for his *Paradise Lost.*

Macbeth Ironically, in his last moment Faustus panicked and confessed his sins. But alas, too late! He wanted all the good things the ancient world could offer, riches, beauty, power, and so on. I can hear the self-mocking lamentations of Cardinal Wolsey: "Vain pomp and glory of this world I hate ye. . . . And when he falls, he falls like Lucifer./ Never to hope again." Faustus merely followed the path paved by our first parent Adam. What moves us in the dark tragedies is the way poetry sublimates human suffering into something noble and poetic.

Richard Into something noble and poetic? Dear Macbeth, you are deceiving yourself. This is no more than mere rhetoric critics enjoy using. It has no bearing on reality, just rubbish.

Macbeth What do you mean, Richard? Critics are guides to readers. How can you be so disparaging and dismissive? I sometimes think you enjoy being a tease.

Richard I just hate their highbrow rhetoric, that's all.

Macbeth Your audacity amazes me. Let me tell you, critics are of invaluable help in making us think and enlarge

귀한 존재들일세. 예술 세계는 냉정하다네. 평론가들이 작품을 인정해 주지 않으면 작가 혼자, 제아무리 잘났어도 소용이 없어요. 작품은 작품이 말해주니까. 셰익스피어가 처음 등장했을 때 그를 엉터리 촌뜨기라고 조롱하던 로버트 그린은 지금 어딨나? 문인들과 평자들로부터 인정받지 못하고, 혼자서 잘났다고 떠벌리던 그자의 극이 무대에 오르기나 하나? 물론 그가 셰익스피어를 시기해서 떠든 소리겠지만.

리처드 아이고, 형님! 알았으니, 여기 물 드시고 진정하시오. (*물병을 건넨다.*) 형님도 알다시피 셰익스피어 주변에는 벤 존슨처럼 그를 칭송한 자들이 많이 있었다오. 그러나 누구보다도 진정 그를 알아본 가장 힘 있는 평자가 누군지 아시오?

맥베스 그게 누군데?

리처드 관객입니다. 그런데 말이오. 20세기 중엽부터 지금까지 문화계를 분탕질하고, 인류의 보편적 가치 기준과 정신세계를 타락시킨 말살 주의자들이 누구요? 인간의 존엄성을 해체하고 가정을 으깨버리겠다고 파괴의 노래를 부르는 자들이 누구요? 지성인의 탈을 쓴 사기꾼 지식인들- 그들

our horizon. The world of arts is a harsh one. If you don't get their approval, no writer can succeed, however good. But then a truly great work speaks for itself. When Shakespeare first started writing, Robert Greene called him a country- bumpkin, but where is Greene now? His contemporaries didn't think much of him, though he himself thought otherwise. None of his plays are ever performed nowadays. What he said of Shakespeare all stems from envy.

Richard All right, all right, don't get so excited now. (*Giving him a bottle of water.*) Here, take a sip and calm down. There were some, like Ben Jonson, who thought highly of Shakespeare, you know. But do you know who the most powerful critic was, who recognized Shakespeare's genius?

Macbeth Who?

Richard The audience. They got it right, but the worst lot, the quarrelsome, contentious, fractious lot, who's been at work since the middle of the twentieth century, who undermined the arts and all the values and achievements of man, do you know who they are? Who wanted to deconstruct human dignity, the family and what not, and sang the paean of destruction? Fake intellectuals, narrow and arrogant

가운데는 편협하고 교만한 대학교수들과 비평가들 책임이 크다는 것만 알아두시오. 인간이 창조 질서를 파괴하는 까닭에 산천초목도 탄식하는 거요.

맥베스 아이고, 진정하시게. 골 아프다! 이보게, 내 결론은 이것이네. 비극적 고통이 영혼의 성장으로 변화시켜주지만, 지나친 욕망으로 인한 파우스트 박사의 고결함이 낭비되어 안타깝다, 이 말을 하고 싶었던 거네.

리처드 형님, 인간은 본질상 진노의 자식이라고 성경은 말하고 있소. 그러나 하나님은 한 생명의 영혼이 온 천하보다 귀하다고 가르칩니다. 내가 저지른 행위를 생각하면 나도 무섭고 떨리오. 하나님이 날 오라 하였소. 그분이 대화하자고 날 불렀소.

맥베스 뭐? 자네가 모세야?

리처드 "오라 우리가 서로 변론하자. 너희의 죄가 주홍 같을지라도 눈과 같이 희어질 것이요. 진홍같이 붉을지라도 양털같이 희게 되리라." 끝내주게 멋진 말씀 아니오? 그분이 죄인 중의 죄인인 우리를 부르고 있소. 우리를 죄에서 자유롭게 놓아주려고 말입니다. 너와 내가 서로 변론하자. 얼굴을 맞대고 대화로 풀자. 이거 아니오? 개인의 자유와 권리를 존중하는 민주적인 접근 아닙니까? 내가 자복하면 내 허물을 씻어주고, 내 죄를 기억지 않겠다고 하였소. 그래서 내가 천국

scholars and critics. It seems that humans are bent on destroying God's creation. No wonder nature is crying out loud.

Macbeth Calm down, dear boy, calm down. All I wanted to say is that suffering is supposed to be ennobling, but it's a real shame that noble Faustus should have been lost because of his ambition.

Richard The Bible says that man is an offspring of wrath, and God says a soul is more precious than the whole world. When I think of my deeds, I shake in fear. I'll tell you what. God once called me, called me for a chat.

Macbeth What! Have you now turned Moses?

Richard "Come now, and let us reason together, saith the Lord: though your sins be as scarlet, they shall be as white as snow; though they be red like crimson, they shall be as wool." Wonderful words, these. He is calling us, you and me, the sinners, to free us from the shackles of our sins. Let's reason together, let's talk face to face. Isn't this approach democratic, showing respect for human dignity and freedom? If I repent, he will wash away my sins, not remember them any more. That's why I can hope for Heaven.

을 바라보는 거요. 형님, 우리 언제 셰익스피어 어른을 방문합시다.

맥베스 그 어른 전도하려고?

리처드 형님도, 참! 전도라면 우리가 그 대상일 거요. 난 그 어른한테 따질 게 많아요. 내가 악한 짓 한 건 인정하오. 우리 어머니도 내게 말했소. 사납고, 무모하고, 거칠고, 난폭하고, 교활하고, 비열하고 잔인한 놈이라고, 태어나지 말았어야 할 놈이라고, 날 낳은 건 쓰라린 업보라고, 우리 어머니가 그렇게 말했다고 셰익스피어가 쓰고 있소. 나도 그런 고약한 나를 동정하지 않습니다. 그렇지만, 셰익스피어의 역사 왜곡은 좀 지나쳤소이다. 앙주의 마가렛 왕비는 그 당시 프랑스에 망명해 있었소. 영국에 있지도 않은 그 저주의 명수, 마귀할멈을 우리 어머니와 우리 형수 앞에 앉혀 놓고 나를 떡을 치고 저주를 퍼붓게 하다니! 난 억울한 바가 있소.

맥베스 자네 무슨 배짱이 그리 두둑한가? 자네의 악행을 작가 셰익스피어 탓으로 돌리려는 건가? 아무리 냉소적이라 해도, 자네 손에 남편들 잃고 자식들 잃고, 거기다 자네는 아내 앤 부인까지 독살했다는 소문이 자자했네. 그 여인들의 애가는 하나도 나무랄 게 없다고.

리처드 셰익스피어가 튜더 신화를 강조한 홀린쉐드 기록에 따라 나를 악귀로 과장해서 묘사한 건 인정하오.

But let's leave such matters and go and pay our dear Shakespeare a visit.

Macbeth So now you want to go and convert him?

Richard I convert him? It's us who need to be converted. But I must say I have a quarrel or two to pick with him. I admit that I've done bad things. Even my mother said I was proud, subtle, sly and bloody, that my birth was a grievous burden, that I was born to make life hell for her. Shakespeare wrote all that. If true, I myself don't feel any sympathy for such a being. But Shakespeare, he went too far. For instance, you know Margaret of Anjou was in exile in France at that time and not in England, but Shakespeare made that witch sit before my mother and sister-in-law to curse and vilify me. He wronged me there.

Macbeth You have the cheek to blame Shakespeare for your infamous deeds! There were rumours everywhere that you poisoned Lady Anne, and what about the cries of women who lost their husbands and children because of you.

Richard According to Holinshed, Shakespeare wanted to endorse the Tudor myth by vilifying me and I think he was right.

맥베스 그러나 자네가 못마땅해 하는 그 여인들의 얘가는 장미 전쟁의 역사를 요약해 준 걸세. 마가렛 왕비는 인과응보의 복수의 여신, 일종의 네메시스 역할로 필요했으니까. 역사적 정확성에 어긋나고 사실보다 과장된 건 나도 인정하겠네. 홍장미 랭커스터 집안과 백장미 자네의 요크 집안, 두 가문의 갈등은, 이를테면 <로미오와 줄리엣>의 몬터규와 캐풀렛 두 집안싸움과 같은 걸세. 그리고 이 사람아, 셰익스피어를 이해해야 하네. 그 사람은 역사를 기술하는 게 아니라, 역사적 진실성에 공헌하고 있는 작가일세. 역사의 자료를 이용하고 응용해서 자기가 의도하는 바를 만들어 내는 칵테일 기술자라고. 극작가로서 그만한 왜곡은 필요한 것 아닌가?

리처드 그게 무슨 칵테일이오. 말이 비단이지, 그건 이도 저도 아닌 짬뽕이오.

맥베스 칵테일이나 짬뽕이나, 뭐가 달라? 그게 그거지. 이 사람아, 두 가문이 30년 동안 벌여온 권력 투쟁. 불법으로 찬탈한 권력이 정당화되고 신성화되는 게 옳으냐? 통치자가 어떻

Macbeth You may not like these women's lamentations but they tell you in a nutshell what the Wars of the Roses were all about. Shakespeare needed a goddess of revenge, a kind of nemesis, and Queen Margaret fitted the bill. But I agree there are some distortions and exaggerations in his handling of history. The quarrel between the two houses, between the red rose of Lancaster and the white of York, is rather similar to the quarrel between the Montagues and the Capulets in *Romeo and Juliet*. My dear Richard, you've got to understand what Shakespeare was trying to do. He wasn't writing a chronicle. He was a playwright trying to make a point about what he understood to be the significance of historical context. He took historical facts and used them to suit his purpose, making them into a kind of melange, a concoction, and as a creative writer, I think he should be allowed that much freedom.

Richard A concoction! A fine word but it means nothing but a jumble.

Macbeth What difference does it make what words you use? The questions Shakespeare raises are these: Is it right to justify an unjust usurpation and a power struggle that went on for thirty years? How does a

게 권력을 잃고 얻느냐? 권력 이동을 탐색하면서 메시지를 던지는 게 셰익스피어의 사극일세. 난 그만한 왜곡은 작가의 특권이라고 생각하네. 아버지가 아들을 죽이고 아들이 아버지를 죽이는 끔찍한 내란을 종식시킨 지도자. 황폐한 나라를 고치기 위해 탄생한 튜더 왕조의 헨리 7세로, 리치먼드 백작이 등극했으니, 위대하지.

리처드 형님도 셰익스피어 작가의 눈에 비친 리처드 3세를 벗어나지 못하는구려. 민중은 어리석기 짝이 없소. 그들이 믿는 자가 "내 말을 따르라" 하면 "옳소" 하고 떼창 부르며 따라갑니다. "죽여!" 하면 죽이고, "찔러!" 하면 찌르고. 옳은지 그른지, 맞는지 틀리는지 조사도 확인도 없이, 무조건 따라갑니다. 형님, 내 몸을 보시오. 내가 꼽추요? 내 등에 혹이 있소? 등이 약간 휘었을 뿐, 두드러진 혹이 있냐고요? 없잖소! 난 어린 시절 알 수 없는 원인으로 팔이 뒤틀리고 어깨 한쪽이 위로 솟는 병에 걸렸소. 그래서 다리 길이도 짝짝이로 이렇게 절름발이가 된 거요. 21세기에 내 유골을 찾았소. 세상을 흔들어 놓은 뉴스를 형님도 잘 알잖소.

맥베스 레스터시의 어느 주차장 밑에서 고고학자들이 리처드 3세의 유해를 발견했지. 학자들이 자네 무덤을 확인했고, 시

ruler gain and lose power, how do power-shifts occur? These are what he wanted to know and asked in his histories. I think a writer has a right to some freedom, that's his privilege. A father kills the son, a son kills the father – the man who brought an end to such doings and delivered the country from waste and devastation, that great man is Henry Tudor, Earl of Richmond, later Henry VII.

Richard I see that you also can't see beyond the Richard that Shakespeare created. As you well know, the mob is foolish. If a man they happen to trust says, "Follow me" they all shout "Yay" and troop after him. If he says, kill, they kill, stab and they stab. They don't think for a minute whether it's right or wrong. They just follow blindly. Look at me. Am I a crook-back? Does my back protrude? No! When I was a child, for some unknown cause, my arms got all twisted and a shoulder shot up. So one of my legs became shorter, and I became a cripple. But in the 21st century they found my body. But you know all about that momentous news.

Macbeth Oh, I heard all about that. Archaeologists dug up under a parking lot in Leicester the remains of what they thought was you, and later verified as you. It

에서 장례식까지 거하게 치러준 역사적인 행사, 나도 물론 알고 있지.

리처드 그 점에 대해 난 레스터시에 감사하고 있소. 내 신체는 감식 결과 척추 측만증으로 판정이 났소. 작가가 그려준 대로 내 등이 그렇게 튀어나오고 몸이 뒤틀렸으면, 내가 즐기는 수영이 가능키나 했겠소? 튜크스베리 전투에서는 어찌 맹렬하게 싸워 공을 세울 수 있었겠냐고요? 이건 모두 내 시신을 발굴해서 확인하고 증명된 사실이오. 셰익스피어는 어째서 거짓된 소리를 덧붙인 거요? 그 이유가 뭐요? 내가 어머니 배 속에서 꼽추로 태어났다면서, 태어날 때부터 머리카락이 어깨에 치렁거렸다느니, 이빨은 모두 솟아 있었다느니, 이거 괴물 아니오? 비틀린 내 심성이 벌 받은 탓에 그런 아기가 태어났다고? 아기가 태어나기도 전에 배 속에서부터 악한 짓을 했다는 거요? 우리의 위대한 극작가가 내게 찍어준 낙인 하나는 영원히 변치도 않소. 이만하면 끝내주는 불멸의 초상화 아닙니까?

맥베스 셰익스피어가 왜 영국 사극을 썼는지 그 큰 의미를 생각해보게나. 군중 심리는 갈대처럼 흔들린다는 자네 지적은 일리가 있네. 잭 케이드가 이끄는 공포의 민중 반란 사건

was a big piece of news that got the whole world excited. They gave you a grand funeral too.

Richard I thank the town of Leicester for that. They examined me and diagnosed my deformity as spinal scoliosis. If my back had been as crooked as Shakespeare had made it out to be and my body as deformed, how could I have enjoyed swimming as I did? How could I have fought so fiercely at the battle of Tewkesbury? Now that they've found my body, they were able to prove that I'm no such monster. But why did Shakespeare tell such lies? For what purpose? He said that I was born a crook-back, that at birth my hair fell down to my shoulders, and I had all my teeth, a veritable monster, no less. He said I was born as such, and it was punishment for my twisted nature. That's what he said. Was he suggesting that an infant did evil in his mother's womb? It's absurd, but the picture the great man stamped me with will never change, an immortal portrait of Richard III.

Macbeth I understand your grievance, but just think about why Shakespeare wrote histories. The populace sways with times as you said. Look at the case of Jack Cade's rebellion and the terror it caused, or the

이나, 『줄리어스 시저』에서 폭도로 변한 시민들이, 음모자 시너와 이름이 같다는 이유로 시인 시너를 죽이는 장면. 공포지. 끔찍하고말고. 폭력적이면서 어처구니없는 이런 장면들은 변덕스럽고 우습기도 한 민중의 모습을 잘 드러내는 대목들이야.

리처드 셰익스피어가 블랙 코미디의 원조라니까요. 로마 시민들을 그렇게 폭도로 몰고 간 게 누구였소? 바로 부르터스를 쓰러트릴 목적으로 연단에 올라선 안토니의 연설 아니었소? 그자가 불붙인 거요. 그자의 말재간이 군대의 힘만큼이나 크다는 사실을 증명한 거요. 설득력 있는 웅변술은 권력을 쟁취하는 열쇠가 되기도 합니다. 나 리처드 글로스터 공작도 왕관을 쓰기 위해서 생각 없는 군중을 요리조리 갖고 놀았으니까요. 그런데 나의 진정한 모습을 셰익스피어 어른께서 피해 간 것 같아 안타깝고 섭섭하다는 말이오. 악인의 가면을 벗은 리처드 글로스터의 소리에는 왜 귀를 기울여 주지 않았느냐, 그 말이오.

맥베스 가면이라니? 악행을 범한 진짜 모습이 자네가 아니었다고?

리처드 전쟁을 눈앞에 두고 내가 나에 대해 느꼈던 영적 불모의 감정은 형님이 느꼈던 것과 비슷할 겁니다. 날 따르는 신하 하나 없고, 내가 죽어도 동정할 자 아무도 없는 내 처지. 형님이 느꼈던 것도 이런 캄캄한 절망감 아니었소? 난 무너

citizens turning into an unruly mob in *Julius Caesar*. You know they massacred poet Cinna because he unfortunately happened to have the same name as the intriguer Cinna, a gruesome scene. These violent and absurd scenes tell you all about the fickleness and unruliness of the mob.

Richard Oh, Shakespeare was the originator of black comedy, I know. But who turned the Romans into such a frenzied mob? Who but Anthony and his speech aimed against Brutus. He set them afire. It proved that words can be mightier than an army. Eloquent and persuasive words are the keys to power. I, Richard, Duke of Gloucester am all too aware of this, and did my part in manipulating the mob to suit my purpose. But I think Shakespeare missed the real me, and that saddens me. Why ignore Richard of Gloucester without his mask?

Macbeth A mask? Do you mean to claim that the villainous Richard isn't real you?

Richard The sense of spiritual devastation I felt before the battle is probably similar to what you had once felt. I had no subject left, none, and no one to grieve over my death. Didn't you feel the same dark despair? I wanted to hide my despair with a shield.

지는 내 마음을 무기로 가리고 싶었고, 약해지는 내 모습을 숨기려고, 방패를 휘두르며 덤빈 것이오. "양심이란 겁쟁이들이 하는 소리다, 굳센 두 팔이 우리의 양심이고, 칼이 우리의 법이다." 나도 형님처럼 이렇게 외쳤소. 두려움이 없었다면 무엇 때문에 그렇게 큰 소리로 요란 떨 필요가 있었겠소? 난 말입니다. 내가 잉글랜드 왕관을 손에 넣기까지, 나와 왕관 사이에 여러 사람 처치했소. 그 왕관을 손에 넣으려고 밤마다 진땀 흘리며 탈진했소. 가시 돋친 숲속에서 길을 잃고, 가시에 찔리며 이리저리 길을 찾아 헤맵니다. 어둠 속에 길은 보이지 않고, 공포에 시달리다, 소스라쳐 놀라서 깨어나곤 하였소. 내가 깜깜한 지옥을 헤맨 거요.

맥베스 자네와 내가 겪은 고통의 시간은 단테의 지옥을 연상시키는군. 자네에게도 비극적 요소가 보이네. 하나에 집착하는 탬벌린의 열정을 닮았어. 그대가 크리스토퍼 말로를 좋아하는 이유를 알 것 같군.

리처드 셰익스피어가 그려준 리처드 3세는 참혹하게 끝났지만, 그러나 난 내 생애의 마감을 단테처럼 긍정적이고 낙관적인 희극 세계의 인물로 끝내고 싶소. 그렇소. 형님 말대로, 장미 전쟁을 종식시킨 리치먼드 백작은 위대하오. 인정합니다. 장미 전쟁의 종식과 더불어 중세도 끝난 것이오. 그런데, 형님께서는 내 마음을 알아주지 못하는 것 같소.

So I wielded it like a sword and fought. "Conscience is but a word that cowards use/ Our strong arms be our conscience, sword, our law!", I cried, just as you might have done. If it wasn't fear, what could have caused me to cry out so loudly? You know, before I got the English crown on my head, I did away many who came between me and it. Every night I would sweat and struggle to reach it. I would lose my way in a thorny path, and wander about here and there getting pricked. I wasn't able to see the path, and would shake in fear. Then I would suddenly wake up. It was in hell that I was wandering about.

Macbeth What you and I went through reminds me of Dante's hell, and I begin to see some potential for tragedy in you. You have something of Tamburlaine in your single-mindedness. Now I see why you are so keen on Marlowe.

Richard Shakespeare's Richard died a bitter death, but I want to end my life as a character in a comedy, in something positive and optimistic like in Dante. You're right to say that it was noble of Richmond to put an end to the Wars of the Roses. I pay him that tribute. It brought the Middle Ages to an end too. But to tell the truth, I don't think you quite understand me, Macbeth.

맥베스 열 길 물속은 알아도 한 길 사람 속은 모른다더니, 자네를 두고 하는 말 같군.

리처드 내가 권좌에 있는 동안엔 말입니다. 2년의 짧은 기간이었지만, 그래도 내 임무에 충실했소. 내란으로 어그러진 나라를 보수하고 백성들을 위한 법안과 정책들을 내놓았소. 인두세 폐지, 죄수 개인의 권리 보장, 조세 체계의 개혁. 평민들의 권익에 신경 쓰고 사법권이 공평하게 처리되도록 노력했소. 문장 인가의 업무를 다루는 문장원도 국가 이래 최초로 내가 창립했고. 당시 경제 최대 강국 이탈리아의 상권에서 우리 산업을 보호하려는 조치도 취했소. 이만하면 잘한 거 아니오? 이런 건 왜 밝혀주지 않았느냐, 그게 섭섭하다는 겁니다.

맥베스 훗날, 울지 추기경도 자네를 가리켜 악을 행한 왕이었지만, 좋은 법을 많이 만들었다고, 리처드 3세를 인정했네. 그러나 여보게, 셰익스피어는 자네의 전기를 쓰려는 게 아니잖은가. 작가의 목적과 소재가 따로 있었던 거지.

리처드 그 어른이 튜더 신화의 선전을 위해서 나의 악행을 과장해서 그렸다면, 장미 전쟁의 통일을 이룩한 리치먼드의 공로에 대한 극은 왜 쓰지 않은 거요? 이 나라 역사를 극화한 셰익스피어가 진정 튜더 신화를 옹호했다면 말입니다. 그렇다면 나를 작살내고 올라선, 튜더 왕조의 첫째 왕에 대한

Macbeth Well, they say you can fathom the depth of a water but not of the heart of a man.

Richard When I was on the throne, in those two short years I did my duty as best as I could. I rebuilt the country torn by civil wars, made laws and policies to help people, abolished the poll tax, improved bail so that felons wouldn't be held illegally, reformed taxation, upheld the rights of commoners, and kept legal justice. I created the College of Arms, and took measures to protect our trade against Italy. Aren't these enough? Then why are these facts not made known? That's what upsets me.

Macbeth Cardinal Wolsey, you know, said you were an evil king but a good legislator. He acknowledged you. But now Shakespeare wasn't trying to write your biography. He was interested in something else.

Richard If he wanted to exaggerate my infamy as part of Tudor propaganda, why didn't he write something on Richmond's achievements? Shakespeare supported the Tudors and their myth, so he should have written a play about the man who crushed me and founded

극은 썼어야 할 것 아니오? 역사는 승자의 기록 아닌가요? 승자 리치먼드 백작, 헨리 7세를 뺀 이유가 뭐요? 헨리 4세, 5세, 6세, 나 리처드 3세까지 주르륵 쓴 작가가, 어째서 헨리 7세는 빈칸으로 건너뛰고, 헨리 8세로 넘어갔느냐, 그 말이오.

맥베스 그건 리치먼드를 주인공으로 발전시키기에는 성격적 매력이 약했던 탓이 아닐까? 극을 창조하고 꾸미는 작가의 눈에는 리처드 글로스터, 자네처럼 화끈하게 끌리는 인물이 있어야 하네.

리처드 형님의 논리는 맞지 않소. 나를 과장해서 포장할 수 있었다면, 리치먼드의 모범적인 선한 행실도 잘 그려낼 수 있었을 거 아니오? 작가의 휘날리는 필치로 멋들어진 쾌걸 리치먼드를 얼마든지 탄생시킬 수 있고말고.

맥베스 여보게, 셰익스피어를 만나면 헨리 7세를 왜 쓰지 않았나, 직접 알아보게나. 나도 그 어른 만나면, 할 말은 있지만, 그렇다고 극을 수정해서 다시 써달라고 할 수야 없지. 난 5막 5장의 독백으로 만족하고 감사하려네.

a new dynasty. That would have been more reasonable. History is a record of victors, so why leave out the Earl of Richmond, Henry VII, the great victor? Shakespeare wrote on Henry IV, V, VI and me Richard III. He wrote about the whole lot, but when it came to Henry VII, he just skipped over and went straight to Henry VIII. In heaven's name, why?

Macbeth Don't you feel that Richmond lacked something in his character to make him into a hero? From a playwright's point of view, a strong character like yours is more dramatic, and therefore a more attractive choice, don't you think?

Richard That doesn't sound too logical to me. If he can exaggerate to create an arch-villain like me, I'm certain he can do the same with a commendable character. With a stroke of his pen, I'm sure he could have created a lion-hearted valiant hero out of Richmond.

Macbeth Well, if you ever get to meet the great man, ask him why he didn't write Henry VII. In truth, I too have a question or two for him, but as I can't ask him to change the play and rewrite bits of it, I'm satisfied with my soliloquy in Act 5 and am grateful for it.

리처드 형님은 차갑고 근엄하지만 남을 탓하지 않는 덕이 있는 분이오. 예술을 사랑하고, 게다가 용감하기까지 하니, 내가 형님을 좋아할 수밖에. 형님은 진정한 군주 감이오.

맥베스 아서라! 그런 말 들으니 겁난다. 내가 『리처드 3세』에 등장했더라면, 군주 감인 내 목숨이 살아남았겠나? 자네 손에 작살났겠지.

리처드 형님, 내 진심을 몰라주니, 정말 섭섭합니다.

맥베스 이보게, 리처드, 날 보고 자꾸 양심이 바르다, 덕이 있다, 그런 소리 하지 말게나. 듣기 거북하네. 누가 들으면, 웃긴다 그래요. 저자들 초록이 동색이라고, 끼리끼리 잘 노네 하고 비아냥거려요.

리처드 한번 낙인찍히면 구제 불능. 씁쓸합니다. 형님은 햄릿의 의붓아버지 클로디어스처럼 음험하고 계산적이지 않아서 좋소. 권모술수에 능한 교활한 클로디어스.

맥베스 클로디어스는 호감 가는 인물은 아니지. 그러나 행정력과 외교력이 특출한 건 인정해야 하네. 거기다 드물게 보는

Richard You're an earnest and reserved sort of person, but one good thing about you is that you don't try to push the blame onto others. Then again, you love the arts and are valiant as well. No wonder I'm fond of you, Macbeth. You are made of the stuff of a true ruler.

Macbeth Come now, you are trying to embarrass me. If I had appeared in your play, would I have survived, the great ruler you make me out to be? I would have been hacked to pieces at your hand.

Richard I'm sorry you should say that. I'm grieved that you should so mistake me.

Macbeth My dear Richard, you keep on saying I am good and have a conscience and all that, but these words put me ill at ease. If others should hear us, they would mock us, and call us the birds of the same feather flocking together to defend each other.

Richard Once they stamp one as a villain, it's impossible to change one's image. That's the bitter truth. But I like you because you're not as Machiavellian and calculating as Claudius.

Macbeth I know Claudius is not a sympathetic character. But you must admit that he is a master of diplomacy and execution. And then, there's a romantic side to him,

로맨틱한 왕이었어. 형을 죽인 이유가 무언가? 형수를 너무나 사랑했기 때문이라고 레어티스에게 고백하지 않던가? "하늘의 별들이 자기 궤도를 벗어날 수 없듯이, 나도 왕비 곁을 떠나서는 한시도 살 수 없다네." 왕비 거트루드를 진정 사랑한 걸 알 수 있는 멋진 대사지.

리처드 그 멋진 고백을 나도 의심치 않소. 그런데요. 레어티스와 햄릿의 대결 장면에서 그 로맨틱한 사나이가 취한 행동이 과연 어땠습니까? 햄릿을 어떻게든, 무슨 수로든, 죽이겠다고 벼르고 준비해 놓은, 그 술잔 말이오. 그 잔이 독배인 사실을 전혀 모르고 있는 거트루드가 마시려 할 때, 클로디어스 입에서 고작 나오는 소리 좀 들어보시오. "거트루드, 마시지 마오!" 네에— 그가 말하는 사이, 거트루드는 이미 마셨다오. 왕비가 죽을 줄 뻔히 알면서 그냥 보고만 있는 거요? 내가 그 역을 맡았더라면, 그녀가 술잔을 잡기가 무섭게 달려들어, 잔을 빼앗아 버렸을 거요.

맥베스 그리 되면 자네가 극을 망치는 꼴이지. 클로디어스는 양심과 행동이 별개임을 보여준 위선자지만, 그래도 죄의식을 보이고 기도하지 않았는가?

which is a rare trait in a king. Why do you think he killed his brother, the king? It's because he was really in love with Gertrude, as he confessed to Laertes: "She is so conjunctive to my life and soul/ That as the star moves not but in his sphere,/ I could not but by her." Wonderful words that show how he loved Gertrude.

Richard I don't doubt his confession for a minute. But look at the duel scene between Hamlet and Laertes. What did that romantic guy do? He was determined to kill Hamlet by any means, fair or unfair, and to that purpose had prepared a poisoned cup. When Gertrude unknowingly was about to drink it, what did he say? "Gertrude, do not drink!" What a lame thing to say, and of course, before the words were out of his mouth, she had drunk it. He knew it would kill her, but he just looked on. If I had been in his shoes, I would have rushed to her and dashed the cup from her lips.

Macbeth If that had happened, you would have ruined the play, for sure. I know Claudius's action and conscience don't seem to match, that he is a hypocrite, but still he suffered from remorse and prayed, didn't he?

리처드 기도요? 기도는 무슨 얼어 죽을 기도! 그자가 무릎 꿇고 기도하고 일어나면서 뭐라고 하던가요? "내가 한 말은 허공에 날아가고 내 마음은 땅에 그대로 있으니, 마음에도 없는 말이 하늘에 오를 리 만무하지." 강탈한 저장물들을 돌려주지 않고 그대로 껴안고 있겠다. 그러니, 그의 기도발이 꽝임을 스스로 인정하는 거요. 이런 고약한 위선자를 형님은 로맨틱하다고 동정합니까? 개뿔이오!

맥베스 오해하지 말게. 왕으로서의 장점을 지적했을 뿐, 그를 동정한 적은 없네.

리처드 형님은 냉정한 사람이지만, 클로디어스 같은 이중인격자가 아니오. 나는 형님하고는 마음 놓고 무슨 얘기든 할 수 있으니 좋소. 하기야 날 상대해 줄 사람이 형님 말고 누가 또 있겠소? 내가 접근하면 내 그림자만 보고도 모두 삼십육계 줄행랑칠 텐데. 형님, 간밤에 버나드 쇼의 『세인트 조운』을 읽었는데요. 조운을 다루는 태도가 셰익스피어와는 180도 달라요. 쇼의 역사관이 셰익스피어보다 훨씬 넓고 크더이다.

맥베스 자네가 독서광인지는 미처 몰랐네.

리처드 독서광까지는 아니고요. 예전부터 혼자 명상하고 책 읽기를 좋아했소. 왜냐? 사촌들도 내 일그러진 몸을 피했고, 누구도 나하고 놀아주지 않았으니까. 그러다 보니 독서에

Richard Pray? Pray my foot! Don't you remember what he said as he was getting up from kneeling? "My words fly up, my thoughts remain below:/ Words without thoughts never to heaven go." He wanted to keep the stolen goods, and he admits to himself that his prayers were empty. You think he's romantic and feel some sympathy for him. But he's a vile hypocrite, that's what he is, and nothing more.

Macbeth Don't misunderstand me. I was only pointing out his good qualities as king. I never had any sympathy for him.

Richard You're a hard man, but you're not two-faced. That's why I like you and can say anything to you. But then, who would ever listen to me, excepting you. They all run a mile if they saw so much as a shadow of me. Listen, last night I read Bernard Shaw's play *Saint Joan*. Shaw's portrayal of Joan is completely different from Shakespeare's. The way Shaw looks at history is far deeper, I think.

Macbeth I didn't know you were a great reader.

Richard No, not a great reader. Just love reading and thinking by myself. Why? Because my cousins avoided my crooked body, and no one would have anything to do with me. So I got into reading books

취미가 붙었소. 외로움을 책 읽는 것으로 달랜 거지요.

맥베스 자네도 외로울 때가 있었다고?

리처드 내 겉만 보지 말고, 속마음을 좀 읽어주시오. 내가 어렸을 때 나를 가엽게 여긴 친절한 어의가 있었소. 내 팔과 어깻죽지를 바로잡아 보려고 수영을 권하기에, 그때부터 열심히 수영을 했는데요. 찌그러진 어깨는 모르겠고, 정신적인 위안이 컸다오. 그래서 지금까지도 내가 유일하게 즐기는 운동이 수영이오. 형님, 수영 좀 하시오? 물밑에 들어가 보았소?

맥베스 아니, 물에 들어가는 거 별로 좋아하지 않네.

리처드 물밑에 들어가면 세상과 절연된 느낌. 그 평안한 정적이 불안한 마음을 진정시켜 줍니다. 눈을 감고 있으면, 얼굴 없는 고요함, 그 속에서 내 회한의 소리가 들리오.

맥베스 자네처럼 어수선한 사람이 정적을 좋아한다고? 그대가 영 딴사람으로 보이네.

리처드 내가 물속에 있거나 홀로 산책을 할 때면 말입니다. 나 자신에게서 탈출하고 싶은 비명이 들리오. 다시 태어날 수는 없을까? 몸은 죽었으나 흙으로 끝나는 게 아니라, 다시

and that's how I got over being lonely.

Macbeth Are you telling me that you suffered from loneliness?

Richard Don't just look at the outside of me but try to look inside, Macbeth. When I was a boy, there was a kind doctor who took pity on me. He tried to treat my shoulder and recommended swimming. So I took up swimming. I don't know about the shoulder, but it helped me a lot mentally. It was the only sport I really enjoyed. Do you swim? Have you ever been under water?

Macbeth No, I'm not too keen on water.

Richard Under water you feel you're in a different world, completely away from everything, if you know what I mean. You feel a kind of serene silence around you, and that's very soothing. I would close my eyes, and in that faceless silence, I would hear the voice of my remorse and regrets.

Macbeth I can't believe a man who bustles about as much as you can like silence. You're beginning to sound like someone else.

Richard When I'm under water or taking a solitary walk, I hear a cry, a voice within that says that I wish to escape from myself, to be born anew. Though my body is dead, I wish that it won't end up as mere

살아나는 부활의 소망을 꿈꾸게 된다오. 굴욕스러운 나의 어두운 신체, 찌그러진 내 그림자를 내려다보면서, 걷다 보면, 해가 기울어 나를 밟게 됩니다. 마치 나를 처형하듯 한 발 두 발 밟고 걸으면서 나의 죄를 주님의 보혈로 씻어주십사고, 영혼을 구원받고 싶은 소망으로 기도합니다. 그리고 평안을 간구합니다. 나 혼자 숨어서 남몰래 얻는 평안이 아니라, 햇빛 찬란한 대낮에 군중 가운데 즐겁게 활보하며, 온 세상에 알리고 싶은 평안. 하늘에서 내리는 내 영혼을 덮어주는 평안을 갈구합니다.

맥베스 자네나 나나 실상은 기독교 국가의 왕이 아니었는가? 부활 신앙은 전 세계 수천 개의 종교 가운데 유일하게 기독교에만 있는 독특한 신앙 체계야. 부활은 인간의 언어와 인간의 지성으로는 절대 설명이 안 되는 신비지. 지금 보니 자네 독실한 신자일세.

리처드 죄 많은 이 몸이 영혼의 양식을 구하는 소리라오. 난 홀로 있을 때면 나에게 보내는 측은지심의 고별사를 듣습니다.

dust. In fact I dream of the hope of resurrection. As I walk, I look down on my crooked shadow, my humiliating dark body. When the sun begins to set, I find myself stepping on myself. Each step is like the sound of an executioner's axe falling, and I ask the Lord to wash away my sins with his sacred blood. I pray in the hope of my soul's salvation and ask for peace. Not the kind of peace I would enjoy in solitude, but the one I could enjoy in the brightness of the sun, walking joyfully among a crowd, a peace I can share with the whole world. I want a peace from above that would assuage the longings of my soul.

Macbeth Thinking of what you said, it occurs to me that both you and I were kings of Christian kingdoms. Among thousands of religions in the world, the belief in resurrection is unique to Christianity. Resurrection is a mystery that no human language or intellect can explain. It seems to me you're a devout Christian, after all.

Richard It's just my sinful body seeking my soul's salvation. When I'm on my own, I hear a farewell song of compassion sung to myself.

맥베스 자네에게 시인의 면모가 있는 게 확실해. 오늘은 어째 내가 아는 리처드 3세 같질 않다. 영 딴사람 같으이. 수수께끼 인물일세. (페이드아웃.)

Macbeth Richard, my boy, I am convinced there's a poet in you. You don't sound at all like the Richard III I know but quite a different man. You puzzle me. (Fade out.)

[장면 2] 리처드와 맥베스의 대화.

(페이드인. [장면 1]과 같은 장소. 같은 때.)

리처드 맥베스 형님, 이제부터는 정말, 형님과 형수님이 겪은 이야기를 듣고 싶소. 두 분은 내게 연구 대상이오.

맥베스 리처드 3세여, 그대야말로 내게 연구 대상일세.

리처드 난 단순해서 연구할 거리가 없소. 그런데 형님은 참으로 진지하고 복잡한 사람이오. 그래서 비극의 주인공에 어울립니다. 내가 왜 형님한테 관심이 있겠소? 형님의 심리적 통찰을 따라갈 수가 없어서 그래요. 형수님도 대단히 놀라운 여인이오. 형님이 코더의 영주가 될 것이고, 또 왕이 될 것이라는 마녀들의 예언을 부인께 미리 편지로 알렸잖소?

맥베스 운명의 편지! 내 일생일대의 참혹한 대실수!

[Scene 2] Richard and Macbeth talking.

(Fade in. *The same time and place.*)

Richard Listen, Macbeth. Now I want to hear all about what you and your wife went through. I find you both interesting objects of study.

Macbeth Richard, it's you who should be the object of study.

Richard No, no! I'm too simple, and there's nothing to explore in me. But you, you are a serious and complex character, and that's why you make such a good tragic hero. Otherwise, why would I take an interest in you? I can't begin to compete with your deep insight into human psychology. And Lady Macbeth, she is an amazing woman. It was to her you sent that letter about the witches's prophesy, of your becoming the Thane of Cawdor and king.

Macbeth That fateful letter! The greatest mistake in my life!

리처드 부인이 편지를 읽을 때부터, 난 이 여자 정말 무섭구나 싶었소. 형님은 부인을 가리켜 "나의 높은 지위의 사랑하는 파트너인 당신에게 이 사실을 알리오"라고 썼소. 형님이 왕이 될 것이라는 마녀들의 예언이 현실이 되기를 바라는 내심, 이게 형님이 숨기고 싶은 야망 아니었소? 형님의 은밀한 욕망을 부인이 파트너로 실행해 주기를 바란 것 아니오? 덩컨 왕의 살해를 두려워하면서도 독려가 필요했던 남편을 부인은 잘 알고 있었소. 난 역사극의 주인공이지, 비극의 주인공이 아니오. 그래서 비극 세계는 들여다볼수록 복잡하고 풀리지 않는 이율배반, 그런 게 흥미롭소.

맥베스 자네는 내 심리 상태를 해부하려 드는구먼.

리처드 형님은 클로디어스나, 나 리처드 3세처럼, <타이터스 안드로니커스>의 속과 겉이 시커먼 주인공 아론 같은 타고난 살인자가 아니라니까요. 그런데 부인은 형님과는 달라요. 덩컨 왕 일행이 글람즈 성에 도착하기 전에 편지를 받아 보고 난 부인은 즉시 머릿속에서 왕을 죽여 놓았소.

맥베스 내 아내는 야만스러운 살인을 위해서 모성애를 스스로 문질러버렸다네. 그날 밤 덩컨의 살해를 두려워한 나는 거사를 없던 일로 하자고 호소했지만, 아내는 듣지 않았어. "젖 빠는 아이가 얼마나 귀여운지 젖을 물려본 나는 잘 알아요. 하지만 당신처럼 다짐했다면 아기가 쳐다보며 방실방실

Richard When she started reading the letter, I knew she was the one to fear. In the letter, you called her "my dearest partner of greatness". That reflects your hidden desire that the prophesy would come true, the ambition that you wanted to hide. Maybe you wanted your partner to act on your desire for you. She knew only too well that you were afraid to kill Duncan and needed some encouragement. I'm a historical figure, not a tragic hero, and the more I look into the world of tragedy, the more contradictory I find it. That's why it's so fascinating.

Macbeth You're trying to dissect my inner world, I see.

Richard I keep on telling you that you're not like me nor Claudius, born criminals, all black within and without, like Aaron in *Titus Andronicus*. But your wife is different from you. The moment she received the letter, she had Duncan killed off in her head, even before he and others had arrived.

Macbeth My wife crushed any maternal feelings she may have had in her for this brutal murder. That night I was afraid to kill Duncan and told her we should abandon the plan, but she wouldn't listen. "I have given suck, and know/ How tender 'tis to love the babe that milks me:/ I would, while it was smiling in my face,/ Have

웃을 때라도, 이도 안 난 잇몸에서 젖꼭지를 잡아 빼고 내 동댕이쳐서 골을 쏟아 놓겠어요." 이렇게나 무섭게 나를 몰아붙였으니까.

리처드 젖 물고 있는 아기 머리통을 깨트리겠다? 남자는 그래야 한다는 형수님의 주장에 소름 끼칩니다. 젖을 빠는 아기의 부드러움과 살인을 어찌 결부시켜 말할 수 있단 말이오? 하나님은 아이들과 젖먹이들의 입으로 권능을 세운다고 하였소.

맥베스 내 아내만 그런 말을 한 건 아니네. 코리올레이너스 어머니 볼럼니아도 똑같은 말을 했으니까. 승리의 기념비에 입힌 금박보다 피로 얼룩진 얼굴이 더 사나이답다면서, "헥터에게 젖을 물린 헤큐바의 젖가슴보다 그리스인의 칼에 맞아 피를 흘리는 헥터의 이마가 더 멋지다." 이렇게 말하지 않았는가?

리처드 형님, 지금 형수님을 엄호하려는 건 아니지요? 난 이런 여자들이 경이롭지만, 솔직히 무섭소. 맞서기 힘든 끔찍한 부류의 여인들이오. 어미의 젖과 군사의 피를 섞어서 말하다니! 이래서 이 여자들이 망가진 것 아니겠소? 이들의 머릿속에는 성(性)과 살인이 묘하게 얽혀 있소.

pluck'd my nipple from his boneless gums,/ And dash'd the brains out, had I so sworn/ As you have done to this." That's how hard she drove me.

Richard To dash out the brains of a suckling child! It gives me the shivers that anyone could be capable of such brutality. How could she talk of the tenderness of a suckling baby and cold-blooded murder in the same breath! God said it is through the praise of children and infants that he has established a stronghold against his enemies.

Macbeth My wife isn't the only one who said something like that. You know Coriolanus's mother Volumnia, she said something similar. She said a face covered in blood is more manly than the gold that covered a trophy of victory: "The breast of Hecuba/ When she did suckle Hector, looked not lovelier/ Than Hector's forehead when it spit foreth blood/ At Grecian sword contemning." That's what she said.

Richard Surely you're not trying to defend your wife, are you? Such women amaze me, and to be honest, I'm a bit scared of them. They're a terrifying lot, impossible to go against. That's why all went to wrack and ruin. In their heads, sex and murder are all one, all mixed together.

맥베스 무슨 수로 내가 마누라를 두둔하겠는가? 난 왕관은 욕심났지만 살인하기는 정말 싫었다네. 마녀들 수작에 넘어간 나의 어리석음이 그저 한없이 후회될 뿐이네. 난 살인을 저지르자마자 내가 한 시간 전에만 죽었더라도 행복했을 텐데 하고, 절규했어.

리처드 살인을 앞세워 남성성을 강조하다니! 젖을 빨고 있는 아가도 던져 버리겠다는 부인의 그 발상이 끔찍하오. 그런데 형님과 형수님은 왕좌에 오르자마자 서로 반대 방향으로 갔단 말입니다. 왕은 맹렬하게 잔혹해지고 왕비는 미쳐 버리고. 이게 무슨 조화요?

맥베스 자네 말대로 우리 부부는 왕위에 오른 후부터 변했네. 물 한 대야면 손에 묻은 피를 말끔히 씻을 수 있다던 여자가, "오- 아라비아의 온갖 향수도 이 작은 손의 피 냄새를 없애주지 못하는가?" 탄식하며 병들어 갔으니까.

리처드 그건 형님이 잃어버린 감각을 형수님은 그때부터 되찾은 거군요.

맥베스 그랬던 것 같네. 여보게, 자네 살인 얘기 정말 억세게 틀어놓는군. 날 보고 어쩌라고? 내 손에서 계속 피 냄새 맡으라고 강요하는 건가?

Macbeth How is it possible to defend her? I was tempted by the crown, but I really didn't want to kill for it. I have nothing but regrets that I should have been such a fool to have been taken in by those hags's trickery. As soon as I did the murder, I was screaming to myself that I would have been happier to have died an hour earlier.

Richard To egg a man on to a murder by taunting him about his manliness! What a woman and what a thought to dash out the brains of a suckling infant! But I noticed that once you got to the throne, you two went in opposite directions. You as king became more brutal, and the queen, she went mad. What happened?

Macbeth As you say, we changed after we ascended the throne. A woman who once said a little water would wash away the blood, that same woman ended up muttering: "Here's the smell of the blood still: all the perfumes/ Of Arabia will not sweeten this little hand." And she withered away.

Richard She discovered the sensibilities that you had lost, I guess.

Macbeth I think so. But Richard, you persist in talking about murder. Are you asking me to go on smelling blood on my hand?

리처드 형님, 우리 지금 맥베스 형님의 핵심에 다가가고 있소. 비평가들 얘기보다 형님 얘기가 더 중요하오. 텍스트 한가운데서 움직인 당사자니까. 이건 극을 쓴 셰익스피어 손에서도 벗어난 거라오. 비극 장르의 묘미는 바로 여기에 있소. 역사극은 극작가가 써 준 대로 따라가면 돼요. 나 같은 인물은 줄에 매달려 조종당하는 마리오네트, 꼭두각시라니까요. 그래서 내가 나를 왜곡했다고 작가를 비난하고 아우성치는 거요. 형님, 맥베스 부인의 사망 소식을 접한 형님의 심정이 어떠했는지, 이제부터 형님의 진솔한 목소리를 듣고 싶소. 이건 셰익스피어도 형님 마음속에 들어가 보지 않았기 때문에 모릅니다. 작가는 형님에게 대본만 제공했을 뿐이오. 그래서 맥베스 역을 맡은 배우들은 이 모양 저 모양으로 인물 해석에 골을 빼는 거라오. 비평가들이 이 말 저 말 늘어놓는 거, 그거 셰익스피어를 흔들어 볼 뿐이지, 인물의 진정성을 평론가들이 어찌 알겠소? 물론 그들의 해설은 독자들과 배우들에게 도움을 줍니다. 그러나 틀린 소리도 분명 있소. 난 맥베스 본인 입을 통해 직접 듣고 싶단 말이오.

맥베스 이보게, 내가 어째, 정신과 의사 앞에 앉아 있는 기분이 든다. 내 마음 나도 모른다는 소리도 있잖은가?

Richard Listen, Macbeth, we're approaching the heart of your story. What you say is far more important than what critics say because you're the one at the centre of the text. You've even gone beyond Shakespeare's control. That's what makes tragedies so fascinating. In histories, you merely follow what the writer wrote. A character like me is a mere puppet. That's why I've been complaining about distortions. But dear Macbeth, I would be so interested to know what you really felt when you heard of your wife's death. I really want to hear your honest voice. Even Shakespeare can't know, as he can't get inside you. He just gave you the script, and that's all there is. That's why the actors playing your role are tearing at their hair to work out what you're really like. The critics have said this and that, and it only makes Shakespeare worse. What can they know of the true nature of his heroes? It's true that their interpretations help actors and readers, but there are bound to be some wrong interpretations. So I want to know the truth from your own lips.

Macbeth Richard, how can I . . . I feel as if I'm sitting in front of a therapist. Sometimes you don't know your own mind, you know.

리처드 형님! 나도 형님께 나에 대한 온갖, 할 소리 못할 소리 다 털어놓았잖소. 가는 게 있으면 오는 것도 있어야 할 것 아니오?

맥베스 어-휴우-

리처드 어찌 그리 긴 한숨을 쉬시오?

맥베스 한숨부터 나온다. 자네는 나를 안다고 생각하나? 실상은 모르고 있네. 한 길 사람 속을 모른다는 말은 바로 나를 두고 하는 말일세. 내가 자네한테 고백하겠네. 난 왕관은 탐났어도, 살인하기는 정말 두렵고 떨렸어. 치가 떨리게 싫었어. 자네는 나를 클로디어스 같은 살인자가 아니라고? 이중인격자가 아니라고? 그건 자네가 나를 모르고 하는 소릴세. 리처드 3세여, 그대는 내가 숨기고 싶은 내 속을 그렇게도 들추고 싶은가? 나야말로 속이 시커먼 위선자라네. 내가 멋져 보이는 비극의 주인공이라고 했나? 빛 좋은 개살구! 나는 햄릿도, 리어도 못 되고, 오셀로도 못 되네. 사람들은 4대 비극 안에 나 맥베스를 높이 인정하는데, 나야말로 비극의 주인공으로 자격 미달, 탈락생이오! 비극의 주인공 감이라면 개인이나 사회를 좀먹는 야만성에 대한 고뇌와 갈등이 있어야 하지 않겠나? 이를 정복하려는 최소한의 투쟁 정신을 보여야 하는 것 아닌가? "사느냐, 죽느

Richard Look here. I've been honest with you and told you this and that about myself. You should reciprocate, don't you think?

Macbeth (*Sighs deeply.*)

Richard Why such a deep sigh?

Macbeth I sigh because I'm not what you think I am. I don't know myself what I am. When they say you can't fathom a man's heart, that's me they're talking about. I'll confess this to you. I surely wanted that crown, but I was really scared to kill, really hated it. You tell me that I'm not a murderer like Claudius, that I'm not double-faced. You don't know me, Richard. Do you really want to look into my heart and dig out what I want to keep buried? Well, let me tell you, I am a true black-hearted hypocrite. You tell me that I'm a great tragic hero. All nonsense, all fake. I'm no equal to Hamlet, Lear or Othello. People include me among the four great tragic heroes but I don't match up to them. A tragic hero should show some awareness of the savagery within an individual or society, and agonize over the conflicts and discord within, or try to put up a fight to overcome them. But I, Macbeth, am a character who doesn't know a thing about such tragic propositions as "To be or not

냐?" 비극 갈등의 명제도 모르는 자가 바로 맥베스라는 인물일세. 나의 위선을 내 아내는 냉철하게 직시했어. 내가 덩컨 살해에 동조하는 사실을 아내는 조금도 의심치 않았지. 나를 꿰뚫어 보는 여자의 치마폭에 숨어서 시해를 범한 치졸한 놈. 도덕심을 상실하면서 나의 야만성이 드러나기 시작한 거야. 기계적인 살인 물레 위에 올라탄 나는 공포의 맛도 잊었고, 살인의 기억도 잃고, 불길한 얘기를 들어도 전혀 놀래지도 않았으니까. 이쯤 되면 사람이, 사람이 아닌 거지. 인간이 그보다 더 추락할 곳은 없네. 비극의 풀리지 않는 이율배반은, 자네 말대로 속과 겉이 흑과 백처럼 다르다는 걸세. 나의 강한 자의식과 통찰력은 클로디어스와 다를 바 없지. 덩컨을 죽이는 살인 행위는 나의 앞날이 사라질지 모르는 위험성을 알면서도, 그 여파가 어떻게 몰려올지 뻔히 내다보면서 저지른 행위야. 덩컨 살해의 유일한 동기가 뭐냐고? 하늘을 찌르는 가당치도 않은 야망이었네. 내가 그 마녀들을 대적하고 물리쳤더라면, 그것들이 날 피했겠지? 그런데 내가 두 마음을 품었어. 나의 악한 교만이 나를 넘어뜨린 거야. 정작 참회록을 써야 할 사람은 자네가 아니고, 맥베스, 나일세. 자네와 내가 악인이라 해도 우린

to be". My wife saw through my duplicity. She had no doubt that I wanted to kill Duncan. I know she saw through me, but I, like a coward, used her to hide my real feelings and intentions. When I lost claim to all morality, my savage nature began to manifest itself. Hung on a wheel that mechanically churned out murder after murder, I lost the taste of fear, memory of murder, and wasn't even afraid when I heard foreboding news. At that stage, you can say that I no longer had any humanity left in me. I couldn't fall lower than where I had fallen. The great paradox, one that bears no reason, is, as you say, the gulf between what's inside and outside. They were totally at odds, just like black and white. My self-awareness is equal to that of Claudius. I saw clearly the murder of Duncan would have consequences and destroy my life, but I went ahead regardless. And what was the driving motive? My groundless vaulting ambition, that was what it was. If I had withstood the witches and told them to clear out, they would have left me alone. But I was deceitful. My devilish arrogance led to my fall. It's me, Macbeth, who should be writing a confession, not you. We're both villains, you and I, but we're

서로 결이 달라. 자네는 악에 대해 솔직했고, 난 나 자신에게조차 숨겼으니까. 나야말로 엉큼한 위선자, 겉만 번지르르한 회칠한 무덤. 허! 허파에서 껄껄 웃음 터질 일이다! 자네는 고요 속에서 평안을 얻는다고 했나? 홀로 사색하는 걸 좋아한다고 했나? 그럴 수 있는 건 축복일세. 죄를 뉘우치고, 하늘을 그리워하는 자네는 복 받은 거야. 악행을 했어도 솔직히 고백하고, 고민하는 자네 모습이 진정 부럽네. 난 그렇지를 못해. 난 밤이 무서워. 고요한 밤이 무서워서 눈을 뜨지 못하는 저주받은 맥베스! 덩컨 왕을 죽이려고 한발 한발 옮기던 내 발소리가 살아나서 내 심장을 찌르며 매질한단 말이다. 왕이 잠든 옆방에서 "우리에게 은총을 베푸소서!" 하는 두 왕자의 잠꼬대 같은 기도문이 들렸지. 그런데 난 목구멍이 막혀, "아멘" 소리가 나오지 않았어. 내가 "아멘"을 죽였어. 내가 잠을 죽였어. 그날 밤 내 발걸음 소리는 나를 지옥으로 끌고 들어가는 조종이었지. 리처드, 그대에게 평안과 안식을 안겨주는 고요함이 내게는 악몽과 공포의 시간일세.

리처드 죄와 벌을 동시에 감지하면서 범행을 저질렀다니! 형님의 그 직관력이 놀랍고도 무섭소.

made of different stuff. You are honest about your villainy but I, I deceived even myself. I'm a deceitful hypocrite, a tomb painted over beautifully but all rotting inside. It's laughable. Didn't you say you found some peace in silent quietude, that you like thinking alone? To be able to do that is a blessing, do you know? You're blessed to be able to repent and hope for Heaven. You've done evil, but you can confess openly, repent, and suffer over it, and I envy you for that. I can't do that. I'm afraid of the dark. The silence and stillness of the night is fearsome to me, so fearsome that I'm afraid to open my eyes. Acursed Macbeth! The sound of each step I took to Duncan's chamber comes alive again and beats against my heart. In the room next to Duncan's, I heard the two princes cry out "God bless us" in their sleep. I couldn't say "Amen" after them. I killed Amen. I killed sleep. The sound of my footsteps that night was the bell leading me to Hell, Richard. The stillness that gives you peace and rest is for me nightmare and dread.

Richard To commit evil in full awareness of its criminality and the punishment to follow! I find your insight astonishing, and also a bit scary, Macbeth.

맥베스 아내의 사망 소식을 들은 난 그 순간 맥이 풀리더군. "왕비가 돌아가셨습니다." 여보게, 우습지만, 아내를 '왕비'라고 부르는 신하의 소리를 난 그때 처음 들어보았네. 왕비를 왕비라고 부르지 않았던 신하들. 왕과 왕비가 버림받았다는 비참한 표시겠지? 아내의 사망을 처음 들었을 때, 내 솔직한 심정은 나도 같이 죽기를 바랐으니까. 내 일생이 안개처럼 사라지는구나. 내가 바람에 흩어져 버리는 흙먼지로구나. 어느 시인의 표현대로, "시커먼 젖은 나뭇가지에 떨어져 붙은 꽃잎." 아직은 물기가 남아 있지만, 곧 시들어 버릴 얇은 꽃잎 말일세. 그게 내 꼴이었네. 나는 죽은 듯 아무 감각 없이 나무토막처럼 있었어.

리처드 그렇다면, 5막 5장의 독백은 죽고 싶은 형님의 심정을 토로한 건가요?

맥베스 그 독백은 삼류 배우로 전락한 나의 초상화네. "주어진 시간 동안 무대 위에서 활개 치고 안달하다가 곧 영영 잊혀버릴 가련한 배우!" 무대를 한 번 휘젓고 꺼져버리는 처량한 배우처럼, 영혼을 팔아서 얻은 영광이 아무 의미 없음을 인식한 거지. 나와 아내는 광풍에 쓸려 한순간에 사라졌어. 그 독백은 우리 부부의 장례식 엘레지겠지. 아내는

Macbeth When I heard of my wife's death, I suddenly felt weak. "The Queen, my Lord, is dead." It sounds absurd, but do you know that it was the first time I heard her being called queen? My subjects didn't call her queen. I suppose it means we were both rejected as king and queen. To go on, when I first heard of her death, my first honest feeling was I wanted to die too. My life was vanishing like a mist. I was dust blown away in the wind, that's what I felt. As one poet wrote: "The apparition of these faces in the crowd;/ Petals on a wet, black bough." Like thin petals, still wet yet but about to wither away soon, I mean. That was my feeling. So I stood there like a block of senseless wood.

Richard If that's what you felt, can I take your soliloquy in Act 5 as an expression of your death wish?

Macbeth Oh, the soliloquy is a kind of portrait of me, who's fallen to being a third-rate actor, "a poor player/ That struts and frets his hour upon the stage,/ And then is heard no more." I had realized that the glory I had gained at the cost of my soul was meaningless. My wife and I were swept away in the storm and vanished in a second. That soliloquy is the elegy sung at our funeral. I don't think my wife

내가 느끼는 공포를 경험하지 못한 것 같았어. 하긴 우리가 같이 있어도 그 여자 눈에는 방쿼의 유령도 보이지 않았으니까.

리처드 그거야 아들 햄릿에게 보이는 아버지 유령이 어머니 거트루드 눈에는 같은 방에 있어도 보이지 않았잖소.

맥베스 내가 아내를 파트너라고 불렀는데, 우린 달라도 너무 달랐네. 나는 늘 불안 속에 살았어. 그런데 머리가 돌아 버린 건 내가 아니고 그쪽이었단 말이지. "잠든 자와 죽은 자는 그림에 불과해요. 화폭에 그려진 귀신을 보고 두려워하는 건 애들뿐입니다" 하고 큰소리치던 강철 같던 여자가 죄의식에 빠져서, 손에 묻은 피에 사로잡히다니! 핏자국을 없애려고 잠도 안 자고 손 씻는 시늉에만 집착하다니! 인간이 한순간 유리알처럼 바싹 깨질 수 있는 약한 존재임을 실감했네. 때로는 귀찮았던 사람. 내 마음 한편에서는 저러고 미쳐 다니느니 차라리 죽어주었으면 하고 은근히 바라던 여자. 그런데, 정작 아내가 죽었다는 소식을 들으니, 그저 앞이 캄캄할 뿐이었어.

리처드 인간은 강하지만 무너지기도 쉬운 기묘한, 불가사의한 존재요. 왜 그런지 아시오? 우린 피조물이라서 그렇소. 완전무결한 조물주 신이 창조한 피조물이라 불완전한 거요. 이 절대 원리의 질서를 무시했기 때문에 파우스트가 엄청난

felt the fear that I felt. She couldn't see Banquo's ghost though she was right there.

Richard Hamlet could see his father's ghost but not Gertrude, though they were in the same room.

Macbeth I called my wife my partner, but in truth we were totally different. I always lived in fear. But it was she who went mad, not me. A woman who had once said, "The sleeping and the dead,/ Are but as pictures; 'tis the eye of childhood/ That fears a painted devil." A strong woman like that falls into a pit of remorse, and gets obsessed with bloody hands, spends sleepless nights walking about trying to wash the blood off her hands! Seeing her made me realize how frail we are, just like a piece of brittle glass. Sometimes I found her a nuisance, and in one corner of my mind, I wanted her dead rather than see her in her madness. But when I heard that she was actually dead, the shock left me wheeling.

Richard Man is a strong creature but easily broken, an inexplicable creature. Do you know why, Macbeth? It's because we are creatures. We're created by the perfect Creator, and our being created makes us imperfect. This is one infallible truth that Faustus

대가를 치른 거 아니겠소? 형수님은 자기가 저지른 짓이 후회막급했던 것이고, 형님도 후회가 컸지요. "해신 넵튠의 큰 바다가 내 손에서 이 피를 씻어낼 수 있을까? 아니다. 오히려 이 손이 광대한 저 푸른 바다를 핏빛으로 물들여 온통 벌겋게 만들 것이다." 대단한 웅변이요, 기막힌 수사요. 맥베스 형님은 끝내주는 시인이오.

맥베스 씻을 수 없는 우리 부부의 죄. 지울 수 없는 그 피가 우리를 놓아주지 않았으니까. 허망한 미래에 우리 두 사람은 똑같이 절망한 거지. 난 비극의 주인공 될 자격이 없네. 내 인생의 지피에스가 잘못되었구나, 실감하고 실패를 깨달아야 비극의 주인공 값이 있는 것 아닌가? 그런데 난 이미 잘못 설정된 지피에스를 알면서 시작했어. 멈추지 않았네. 뻔히 내다보면서 달렸는데, 거기에 무슨 갈등이 있었겠나? 무슨 감동이 있겠나?

리처드 "언젠가는 죽어야 할 여인. 언젠가는 그런 말을 들어야 할 때가 올 것이었다." 형님 독백의 이 첫 마디를 들었을 때 받은 인상은 몰인정하고 매정하게 들렸소. 그런데 그다음 이어지는 대사가 나를 깊은 심연으로 끌고 갑디다.

맥베스 결국 마녀들의 애매한 언사 때문에 내가 망한 거지. 마녀들의 애매한 언사는 언어상의 허위야. 내가 그 허위에 넘어간 거네.

ignored, and paid for. Lady Macbeth was full of guilt for what she had done, and you too. "Will all great Neptune's ocean wash this blood/ Clean from my hand? No, this my hand will rather/ The multitudinous seas incarnadine." What lines! What eloquence! Macbeth, you are a great poet!

Macbeth We committed unforgivable sins, and the blood we shed couldn't be washed away and held us captive. Thinking of the hopeless days ahead, we both fell into despair. I'm not worthy to be a tragic hero. A tragic hero reaches a recognition that something is wrong, that he is failing, and the GPS of his life is going all awry. But I knew beforehand that my GPS had been set wrong from the start, and knowing it, I still went ahead. I knew clearly what lay ahead, but persisted. What conflict is there, what's uplifting about it?

Richard "She should have died hereafter:/ There would have been a time for such a word." These first lines of your soliloquy sounded a bit cold and unfeeling. But what came next really moved me deeply.

Macbeth Well, the witches's prophesy brought about my fall. I was completely taken in by their equivocal words, their empty words.

리처드　모호한 말은 불신의 냄새를 풍기지요. 애매모호한 건 언제나 위험한 거라오. 형님 같은 이상주의자는 브루터스처럼 음모에 잘 넘어가는 결함이 있어요. 그런 약점을 마녀들이 이용해서 형님께 접근한 것 같소. 알고 보면, 꿈이 있어서 속은 거요.

맥베스　꿈이 문제 될 거야 없지. 자네처럼 왕 될 꿈만 꾸면서 사람도 웃으면서 죽이는, 그런 게 고약한 꿈이지.

리처드　꿈이 많으면 헛된 것도 많다고 솔로몬이 그랬소. 그래도 꿈은 좋은 거라오. 사람을 메마르지 않게 지켜주는 하늘의 선물이오. 아동 책이 대부분 꿈 얘기 아니오? 꿈이 인류를 구원하는 원동력이 되는 건 진리요. 요셉도 꿈 한방에 세계 기근을 해결했잖소?

맥베스　하기야 꿈이 무슨 죄가 있나? 파멸의 결과를 뻔히 알면서 품은 내 욕망이 문제지.

리처드　그렇소. 형님은 세상에 어둠을 부르는 욕망을 키웠소. 형님한테는 좀 미안한 얘기지만, 어찌 보면 이건 익살스러운 해프닝 아니겠소? 눈뜨고 노상강도한테 털리듯, 들판에 숨어 있다 나타난 마녀들에게 사기당한 꼴 아니오? 냉철한 맥베스 장군이 농락당하고 쓰러지다니!

Richard Equivocal ambiguous words lead to distrust, and ambiguity is always dangerous. An idealist like you are bound to get entrapped, like Brutus. The hags knew that, and so approached you. You were deceived because you had a dream.

Macbeth There's nothing wrong with having a dream. Unless it's like your case, a dream of becoming king and doing away with people with a smile. That's a bad dream.

Richard Solomon once said much dreaming and many words are meaningless. Nevertheless, dreaming is good. Dreams are heavenly gifts that enrich life. Most children's books are about dreams, and it's true that dreams are the driving force of man's salvation. Joseph solved the famine problem through his dream, didn't he?

Macbeth Why blame dreams? I knew perfectly well the outcome would be death and destruction, but my ambition drove me.

Richard You're right, there. You let your dark ambition grow, and that brought darkness into the world. I'm sorry to say this but I find the incident of the witches rather comic. You were conned by those hags. They hid in the wild and robbed you in broad daylight. To see a cool-headed man like you so fooled by them.

맥베스 내 머리가 혼미해진 틈을 그것들이 놓치지 않은 거지.

리처드 형님을 보면서 나 자신을 반추해 보았소. 형님 속마음을 진솔하게 들려주어 고맙소.

맥베스 속을 털어놓고 나니, 외려 홀가분하다. 자네한테 쥐어 짜이길 잘했군. 채찍에 해독된 기분이랄까? 리처드 3세여, 내 말벗이 되어 주어 고마우이.

리처드 길을 잃고 헤매던 형님과 내가 길을 찾아 돌아온 겁니다. 결과적으로 형님은 애처가도 공처가도 아니군요. 그러나 나와는 차원이 다른 비상한 분이라는 사실을 알게 되었소. 그거 아시오? 형님은 애정 관념이 없는 분이오. 애정의 불모지. 그런 분이 예술을 사랑할 수 있다는 게 놀랍소.

맥베스 그대는 나의 환부에 일격을 가하는군. 날 해부할 곳이 아직도 남았나? 내가 사랑에 야박한 인간임을 부정하지 않겠네. 자네는 그럼 뭐가 다른가? 자네가 가꾼 풍성한 애정의 꽃나무는 어디 있기나 한 건가?

리처드 난 진정한 애정을 숨겼소이다. 거부당할 게 뻔한지라, 부끄러운 치욕의 상처를 받지 않으려고 자존심이라는 가리

Macbeth My head must have been befuddled then, and they took advantage of that, I suppose.

Richard Well Macbeth. Looking at you has led me to look into myself. Thanks for confiding in me.

Macbeth I feel rather relieved after telling you all this. You did me good to get me to unburden myself. I feel as if poison has been taken out of my system. Thanks for talking to me, dear boy.

Richard We've been wandering around lost, but now I think we're on the right path. To get back to my previous question, it seems you're neither a devoted husband nor a henpecked one. But I see now that you are a man of some substance who belongs to an entirely different class from me. Do you know, I think you're a man who's not much interested in love. In fact, an emotional desert where love is concerned, and it surprises me that such a man can appreciate the arts.

Macbeth That's a sore point that you're touching on. Is there still something more left in me to dissect? I won't deny that I'm ignorant about love. But how are you different, may I ask? Where is the flower of love that you cultivated?

Richard Actually I concealed my true love because I knew that I would be rejected outright. I hid that shameful

개를 내세운 것뿐이오.

맥베스 무슨 뜻이지?

리처드 내 흉측한 신체와 흉악한 내 죄는 사랑의 걸림돌이오. 누가 나를 진정으로 좋아하겠소? 그래서 난 가짜 사랑놀이나 즐겼을 뿐이라오. 형님을 '애정의 불모지'라 해서 기분이 상하셨나 본데, 그럼 내가 단도직입적으로 질문 하나 하리다. 형님은 닭똥 같은 눈물을 흘려 본 적이 있소?

맥베스 눈물이면 눈물이지, 왜 하필 닭똥 같은 눈물이냐? 여보게, 남자는 울면 아니 된다. 이렇게 교육받지 않았는가?

리처드 눈물샘은 여자한테만 있답니까? 로미오가 추방당하고 줄리엣과 헤어지게 되니 바닥에 누워 몸부림치며 울었소. 그러자 로렌스 신부는 남자가 계집애처럼 징징댄다며, 어서 일어나라고 야단쳤지요. 남자는 웃는 건 되고, 우는 건 안 된다는 훈시가 어떤 경전에 쓰여 있답니까? 그건 인간의 본질을 부정하는 잘못된 교육이오. 남자애들이라고 울지 못하게 가르쳐선 안 되는 거요.

맥베스 자네와 나는 지존의 위엄을 지켜야 할 처지에 눈물 바람은 금물이네.

리처드 왕도 사람이오. 리처드 2세는, "나도 경들처럼 빵을 먹고 살고, 부족한 것도 알고, 슬픔도 느끼고, 친구도 필요하다." 그러면서 정벌하러 떠난 아일랜드 흙바닥에 주저앉아 울었소.

humiliating wound by pretending to be proud and uncaring.

Macbeth What might you mean by that?

Richard My ugly body and evil disposition are obstacles to love. Who could ever love me? All I had was the pretense. I am afraid the word desert offended you, but I'll ask you a direct question. Have you ever shed tears, large drops?

Macbeth Tear drops are tear drops, whether large or small. Look here, Richard, you know that we men are taught not to cry.

Richard Why should they think that only women can shed tears? When Romeo was exiled and separated from his Juliet, he rolled on the ground and shed buckets. Friar Lawrence scolded him for weeping like a woman. Men can laugh but not weep, where do you find such a rule? It's contrary to human nature, and boys shouldn't be taught it.

Macbeth We both have to keep up our kingly dignity, so tears are forbidden us.

Richard Kings are men too. As Richard II said, "I live with bread like you, feel want,/ Taste grief, need friends." And he sat on the ground and wept on his way to Ireland.

맥베스 그렇다면 리처드 3세여, 그대는 닭똥 눈물을 흘렸다는 건가?

리처드 난 울보요. 물속에서도 물 밖에서도, 내 행실을 돌아보고 통곡한 자요.

맥베스 여보게, 변명 좀 하자면, 난 태어날 때부터 비정한 인간은 아니었네. 그러나 하나님의 기름 부음 받은 자를 죽인, 용서받지 못할 악을 행한 나 자신에게 너무도 절망했어. 글람즈의 영주로서, 장군으로서 난 행복했네. 거기까지가 하늘이 내게 맡긴 몫이었건만. 왕의 자리는 내 그릇이 아니었건만! 나의 것이 아닌 것을 탐낸 내 죄가 참으로 크다. 이 몸에 맞지 않는, 내 옷이 아닌 걸 훔쳐 입은 내 모습이 초라했어. 마치 의상도 제대로 못 갖춰 입은 삼류 배우 꼬락서니라니! 자네는 죄짓고, 지은 죄를 뉘우치고 새 삶을 갈망했지만, 난 시커먼 죽음 속에 그대로 가라앉아 버렸어. 나의 바싹 마른 나무토막 같은 심장이 눈물샘도 말려 죽인 거지. 이보게, 리처드! 숱한 사람을 이용하고 가차 없이 죽인 자네야말로 사랑을 운운할 자격이 있는가?

리처드 그런 까닭에 피 흘린 죄에서 나를 건져달라고 하나님께 간구하는 것이오. 동냥 그릇 들고 헤매는 굶주린 거지처럼, 하늘의 자비를 애걸하는 거요. 형님을 애정의 불모지라 해

Macbeth Are you by any chance confessing that you had shed large drops of tears?

Richard Oh, I'm a cry-baby. Under water and out of water, I think of my deeds and weep.

Macbeth If I were to make excuses for myself, I'll tell you that I wasn't born as cold-blooded as I seem. But by murdering the anointed one, by committing that unforgivable sin, I fell into despair. As Glamis, as a general I was happy. That's as far as Heaven allowed as mine to enjoy, and the throne didn't belong to me. I coveted what wasn't mine and that was a grievous sin. I stole clothes that didn't belong to me and didn't fit me, and I looked pitiful in them, like a third-rate actor who couldn't get himself properly fitted out for his part. I repented of my sins and longed for a new start, but I sank deeper into darkness, into death. My withered heart dried up my tears. But you, Richard, you who made use of people and killed so many, what right have you to talk of love, I ask you?

Richard I know what I've done, and that's why I pray fervently to be delivered from my bloody sins, like a starving beggar going around begging for alms. I think you're upset that I called you an emotional

서 심히 언짢으신 모양인데, 날 어여삐 굽어보시구려. 형님, 우리 기분 전환으로 다음에 언제 오필리아하고 식사 한번 하면 어떻소? 나한테 오래전부터 간직하고 있는 그녀의 연락처가 있거든요. 아니지! 리처드 3세인 줄 알면, 꺼릴 테니, 형님이 만나보고 싶다 하시오.

맥베스 그럼, 햄릿도 같이 부르자. 혹시 그가 영국에 있다면.

리처드 형님은 햄릿의 뭐가 그리 좋소?

맥베스 인간이란 무엇이냐, 깊이 사색하는 젊은이의 태도가 감동적이네.

리처드 사고뭉치요!

맥베스 사고로 뭉쳐 있는 철학도, 그게 그의 전공인데, 뭘 그러나.

리처드 철학도 맞아요. 그러니 끊임없이 자신의 정체를 찾느라고 질문만 하고 헤매지요. 원래 철학이 그런 거요. 질문만 있고 답이 없는 거라오.

맥베스 질문을 계속하다 보면 답도 나올 수 있는 거네. 그게 철학 아닌가? 자네하고 햄릿이 의외로 서로 잘 통할 수도 있어. 두 사람의 대화를 들으면 재미있을 것 같은데. 괜스레 그에게 경쟁의식 느낄 필요는 없다고.

desert, but please forgive me and let it pass. To change the subject to a more cheerful one, why don't we ask Ophelia for a meal? I have her number from of old. No, that won't do. If she knows it's from me, she'll refuse the call. Why don't you contact her?

Macbeth Let's ask Hamlet too, if he's in England by any chance.

Richard Why do you like Hamlet so much?

Macbeth It moves me to find a young man reflecting deeply on things like what it means to be human and all that.

Richard He is nothing but a troubled and confused young man.

Macbeth Well, his speciality is philosophy, and philosophy is troublesome and confusing.

Richard He's a student of philosophy all right. You know in philosophy there are endless questions, only no answers. That's why Hamlet is endlessly asking questions about himself to no end.

Macbeth Well, if you keep asking, maybe one day you might come up with some answers. I think you two might get on. It might be interesting to overhear your conversation with Hamlet. There's no need for you to see him as a rival, you know.

리처드 대화도 서로 맥이 통해야 하는 거요. 햄릿은 내 스타일이 아니오.

맥베스 스타일이 뭐가 문제야? 자네가 내 속을 들여다보고 싶어 한 것처럼, 왜 복수를 지연했는지, 그 이유를 햄릿 본인 입으로 직접 들어보세.

리처드 아니요. 그의 독백만으로 충분하오. 오해는 마오. 난 햄릿을 높이 평가하오. 머리도 뛰어나고. 문학 속 인물 가운데 오이디푸스 다음으로 두뇌가 제일 우수한 자가 아닐까 생각하오. 햄릿의 한량없이 관대한 성품, 오필리아 표현대로 그의 '고상한 기품'을 인정하오. 고매한 청년, 맞습니다. 난 단지 그의 성격이 마음에 들지 않을 뿐이오.

맥베스 성품은 뭐고 성격은 뭔가? 자넨 날 헷갈리게 하는 재주가 있어.

리처드 형님, 난 햄릿을 보고 싶은 마음이 추호도 없으니, 그 정도로 해둡시다. 그자가 하는 행동에서 내 마음을 불편하게 하는 못마땅한 부분도 있다는 점만 알아두시오. 하지만 오필리아는 달라요. 오필리아를 생각하면 내 마음이 짠하게 아파요. 그 애는 내가 정말 아까워하는, 내가 진정으로 아끼는 아가씨라고 말할 수 있소. 모두 썩어 문드러진, 악취 나는 게임 판에서 유일하게 순수한 여자요.

맥베스 자네가 언제부터 그렇게 순수한 여자를 좋아했나?

Richard You can only talk to someone if you're on the same wave length. Hamlet isn't my type of guy.

Macbeth What does it matter if he isn't? Just as you wanted to find out what I was thinking, aren't you curious why he procrastinated? Let's ask him.

Richard No, no! I've had quite enough of him and his soliloquies. Don't mistake me. I have a high opinion of Hamlet. He's intelligent, second only to Oedipus in brain power among literary characters that I know. Then again, he is sweet-tempered, and I agree with Ophelia about his "noble mind". He is undoubtedly a noble young man. But I don't like his character.

Macbeth What's the difference between mind and character? You confuse me.

Richard Well, my dear Macbeth, all I want to say is, in all honesty I have no desire to see Hamlet at all, so let's leave him at that. As for Ophelia, she's a different matter. Whenever I think of her, my heart bleeds for her. What happened to her is a real pity, and I really value her as the only pure being in the stench of the rotting filth of the Danish court.

Macbeth Since when did you start appreciating pure women?

리처드 놀리지 마시오. 내 진심이오. 그런 환경에서 오필리아는 미칠 수밖에 없었다오. 미치게 되어 있었소. 햄릿처럼 가짜로 미친 게 아니라, 진짜로 미쳐 버렸소. 가엾은 아가씨!

맥베스 오오라! 자네가 햄릿한테 감정이 있는 이유를 이제 알았다. 자네 말대로 내가 애정의 불모지라서 그걸 미처 몰랐네. 오필리아가 답이었는데, 등잔 밑이 어두웠어. 질투심이 작용한 거구먼. 질투심! 그거 무서운 거지. 그래, 어디, 오필리아에 대한 자네 얘기 좀 들어보세.

리처드 형님, 날 콰지모도의 패러디로 만들 셈이오?

맥베스 콰지모도? 셰익스피어에 나오는 인물인가? 어느 작품에 등장하지?

리처드 콰지모도는 프랑스 소설에 나옵니다. 셰익스피어와 관계없으니, 내가 하려는 얘기나 들어주시오.

맥베스 그래, 어디 들어봄세.

리처드 오필리아는 대단히 감성적이고 통찰력 뛰어난 아가씨요. 3막 1장의 그녀의 독백은 시쳇말로 내 심금을 울린다오.

맥베스 "아름다운 종이 깨질 때 쨍그랑 소리를 내듯, 왕자님의 고매하고 뛰어난 이성이 깡그리 깨어지다니. 오 슬프다, 내 신세! 내가 저렇게까지 광기로 변한 왕자님을 보게 될 줄이야!"

Richard Please don't joke about it, I'm serious. In the situation that she was in, she couldn't but go insane. Her madness wasn't faked like Hamlet's. She really lost her mind, poor girl.

Macbeth Oh, now I know why your feelings for Hamlet are none too friendly. I guess my lack of sensibility kept me from seeing it. The answer lies in Ophelia, ha. I should have guessed. It's jealousy, jealousy raising its ugly head, eh? That's a bad case, but let's hear what you have to say about Ophelia.

Richard You're turning me into a parody of Quasimodo.

Macbeth Quasimodo? Is that a character in Shakespeare? In which play?

Richard Quasimodo is from a French novel. He has nothing to do with Shakespeare, so just listen to what I have to say.

Macbeth All right. Go on!

Richard Ophelia is a very sensitive and insightful girl. Her soliloquy in Act 3:1 really got me.

Macbeth "Now see that noble and most sovereign reason/ Like sweet bells jangled out of time, and harsh." Her words.

리처드 형님, 오필리아는 햄릿의 광기를 마치 자기 앞날의 광기인 듯 말하고 있소. 헤큐바의 예언가 딸 카산드라를 연상시킵니다. 카산드라가 아가멤논의 마누라 손에 죽게 될 자신의 앞날을 미리 내다보듯 오필리아도 신비한 소리를 하는 거요. 한마디로, 그녀는 이 비극을 증언하는 말 없는 증인이오. 전체 극 한중간에 나오는 그녀의 독백을 난 르네상스 비극 『햄릿』을 요약해 주는 중심으로 봅니다.

맥베스 미술관에서 존 밀레이의 "오필리아" 시리즈를 감상할 때마다 나도 마음이 우울하고 착잡하다네. 그 아이가 몹시 안쓰러워.

리처드 내가 만일 화가라면 말입니다. 나라면 물 위에서 노래하며 죽어가는 그런 모습 대신에, 어지러운 세상에 눈 감고 물속에 편안히 잠든 청초한 모습으로 그렸을 것 같소. 오늘 밤엔 내가 아무래도 오필리아 유령이라도 안고 자는 게 아닌지 모르겠소. 하하하.

맥베스 누가 자네를 말리겠나! 자네는 오필리아도 좋아하고 코딜리어도 좋아하고, 순수한 여자는 다 좋아하는군그래.

리처드 내가 언제 코딜리어를 좋아한다고 했소? 좋은 여자하고 좋아하는 여자는 별개의 문제요. 형님, 코딜리어는 오필리아처럼 남친한테 선물이나 연애편지 받고 바들바들 새가슴 떨 그런 아가씨가 아니라오. 코딜리어는 옳지 않은 일

Richard Ophelia talks about Hamlet's madness as if she has a premonition of her own. She reminds me of Hecuba's prophetess daughter, Cassandra. Now Cassandra could foresee her own death at the hand of Agamemnon's wife, and Ophelia said something as mysterious. She is a silent witness in this tragedy, and I regard her soliloquy as being at the heart of the play.

Macbeth Whenever I go and look at John Millais's Ophelia in the picture gallery, I feel saddened and feel pity for her.

Richard If I had been the painter, instead of painting her with her eyes half closed, singing her death song, I would have painted her dead, pale, and pure. I have a feeling I might end up sleeping with her ghost tonight, ha ha ha!

Macbeth Who can stop you, Richard! I see that you like Ophelia, Cordelia, in fact all pure and good women.

Richard When did I ever say I liked Cordelia? Liking a woman and finding a woman admirable are two totally different things. Cordelia is not like Ophelia, whose little heart beats at receiving presents and letters from her boyfriend. Cordelia, now, is a

에는 어떤 탄압에도 굴하지 않는, 정복되지 않는 여인. 아버지를 구하려고 프랑스에서 군사 이끌고 바다 건너온 담대한 여전사요. 반면에 오필리아는 순진하게 희생된 아가씨요. 내가 『햄릿』 극에 출연했다면, 오필리아를 그대로 죽게 놔두지는 않았을 거요.

맥베스 자네는 거투르드도 구해주고 오필리아도 구해주고, 햄릿 여자들의 구세주 날 뻔했군그래. 햄릿이나 자네나 오필리아를 좋아하는 거 보면, 두 사람 모두 여자 보는 취향이 비슷한데. 혹시 기회가 있으면, 오필리아에게 마음을 고백할 생각 없나?

리처드 형님, 내가 로렌스의 2행시를 빌려서 대답하리다. "타인에게 사랑을 강요하는 자는 스스로 자신의 몸 안에 살인을 낳는 자이러니."

맥베스 무슨 그런 시가 다 있나? 자네 살인 많이 하더니, 실연하면 자살이라도 하겠다는 거야?

리처드 내가 심약한 순정파로 보이시오? 그리 사람 보는 눈이 없는데 어찌 리처드 3세를 연구하겠다는 거요?

맥베스 자네 그 시야말로 사랑과 살인을 한입에 물고 있는 거 아닌가? 셰익스피어의 주옥같은 연시들은 다 어쩌고?

리처드 "내 그대를 여름날에 비교하리오?" 뭐, 이런 거 말이오? 진정성 있는 여인한테 난 낯간지러워서 그리 못하오.

formidable woman who will never bend to what is not right, however hard pressed. She is a female warrior who led the French army to rescue her father. Ophelia, on the other hand, is a woman who was innocently sacrificed. Simply a victim. If I had played in *Hamlet*, I would never have let her die.

Macbeth So you would have rescued Gertrude, and Ophelia too, the saviour of *Hamlet*'s female characters. You and Hamlet seem to fancy the same type of women. If given the chance, would you have told her of your love?

Richard I'll answer that, Macbeth, by quoting D. H. Lawrence's poem: "And whosoever forces himself to love anybody/ begets a murderer in his own body."

Macbeth What poem is that? After massacring so many, are you about to kill yourself for unrequited love?

Richard Do I look like a mooning romantic idiot? With such lack of understanding, how can you hope to study my character, Macbeth?

Macbeth That poem you just quoted utters love and murder in the same breath. What about Shakespeare's sonnets?

Richard "Shall I compare thee to a summer's day?" You mean something like this? No, I'd be too embarrassed to utter such words before a woman I truly loved.

맥베스 자네, 참 별종이다!

리처드 난 다만 그 아가씨 위로해주고 싶은 마음뿐, 진도 나갈 일 없소이다.

맥베스 어떻게 위로하려는데?

리처드 위로도 예행연습이 필요하오?

맥베스 그러나저러나, 리처드 3세여, 진작부터 궁금하던 터인데, 우리를 여기 이 공원에 불러낸 자는 대체 누군가?

리처드 대한민국 셰익스피어 학회에서 요청이 왔어요. 은퇴한 어느 할매 교수가 그곳 학회 60주년 기념행사 때 형님과 나를 주인공으로 꾸민 대화극을 공연하고 싶답니다. 예사롭지 않은 아이디어라 마음이 끌렸소. 그래, 대뜸 오케이 한 거요. 너무 먼 곳이라 형님께는 무리일 것 같아, 내가 대표로 참석하겠다고 했소.

맥베스 자네가 공연에 출연하나?

리처드 아니지요. 우린 등장인물이고요, 공연은 그곳 배우들이 합니다.

맥베스 아무튼 자네는 발도 넓군. 그 나라는 또 어찌 알았는고?

리처드 형님 귀에는 셰익스피어 대사만 들리고, 지구 돌아가는

Macbeth What an oddity you are!

Richard I merely want to console her and have no intention of going further.

Macbeth Console? How?

Richard For heaven's sake, Macbeth, must I put on a show to make you see how?

Macbeth I have no idea. But leaving that aside, Richard, there's something I'm curious about. Who on earth called us up to this park? Do you know?

Richard Well, Macbeth. I had an invitation from the Shakespeare Association of Korea. Some old lady, a retired professor in fact, wanted to put on a performance of a duologue with you and me in it to celebrate the 60th anniversary of the association. I thought it was a peculiar request, but got interested. So I agreed. Korea is some distance away, so it might be too much for you to go, but I'll go to represent us both.

Macbeth Are you going to perform?

Richard Oh no, we are characters in it. The actors, they'll perform.

Macbeth You seem to know everyone. How did you get to know that country?

Richard Are your interests confined to Shakespeare only?

소리는 안 들리시오? 대한민국을 모르시오? 쏘니, 손흥민의 나라를 모른다는 거요?

맥베스 이보게, 20세기 중반에 치른 막대한 전쟁에도 불구하고, 잿더미 속에서 살아난 불사조 같은 나라, 자유 대한민국. 나도 그 정도는 안다. 오죽하면 소년단 이름을 '방탄'이라 지었겠나? 방송에 나온 어떤 정치 평론가에 의하면 코리아는 새우가 21세기에 고래로 변한 나라라고 하더군.

리처드 그건 코리아 껍데기만 알 뿐, 그 나라의 진정한 생태를 모르고 하는 소리요. 형님, 소위 평론가네, 엘리트네, 하는 교수들 말을 다 믿으면 안 된다고 내가 그랬지요? 웃기는 엉터리가 많다고요. 코리아는 새우인 적이 없어요. 처음 태생부터 고래였소. 작은 고래가 큰 고래로 컸을 뿐이오.

맥베스 자넨 코리아 전문가처럼 들린다. 내가 궁금한 건, 어떻게 그 나라와 자네가 연결이 닿았는지, 그걸 묻는 걸세.

리처드 그곳 학회 지인을 통해서 연락이 왔소. 난 이번 코리아 학회에 은근히 기대하는 게 있답니다. 이번 코리아 방문이 나의 악한 이미지를 씻는 계기가 되었으면 하는 바람입니다.

맥베스 이 사람아, 바랄 걸 바라게. 자네한테는 '악-인' 두 글자가 붙어 다니네. 신분 세탁이란 말은 들어봤어도 이미지 세탁

Don't you know what's going on in the world? Haven't you heard of Korea? Sonny? Son Heung-min and where he's from?

Macbeth Oh, I know that much. A country that was laid waste by war in the mid-twentieth century, and rose like a phoenix from its ashes! The free nation of Korea, the native land of the renowned BTS! According to a political commentator, it's a country that transformed itself from being a shrimp to a whale.

Richard Oh, political commentators know nothing about Korea or know it only superficially. Don't you believe in everything critics, elites or professors, the so-called experts say. Korea has never been a shrimp. It was always a whale, a small one but a whale nevertheless, and it has now grown to be a big whale.

Macbeth You sound like a Korea expert yourself. What I want to know is how they got in touch with you.

Richard Oh, I know someone in the Association. I'm actually expecting some good to come of this visit. I'm hoping it will be an opportunity to whitewash some of my evil image.

Macbeth Richard, dear boy. I think you're harbouring vain hopes. "A Villain", that stigma accompanies you

은 또 뭐야?

리처드 한번 뇌리에 박히면 세뇌 탈출이 쉽지 않다니까요. 빼도 박도 못하는 셰익스피어가 그려놓은 내 초상화. 누구를 탓하리오?

맥베스 그런데 우리 대화극 제목이 뭔가?

리처드 아, 참! 중요한 걸 깜빡했군요. 우리 두 사람 이야기니까 제목은 이쪽에서 정하는 게 좋겠다고 했어요. 뭐라고 하면 좋겠소?

맥베스 자네 알아서 짓게나.

리처드 형님, 그래도 제목은 관록 있는 형님이 정하는 게 좋지 않겠소?

맥베스 제목하고 관록이 무슨 상관이야?

리처드 우리의 첫 코리아 데뷔, 첫 무대인데, 그래도 권위 있는 비극의 주인공, 장래 크리스토퍼 말로의 부친이 될지도 모르는, 맥베스 형님이 지어주는 게 바람직하지 않겠소?

맥베스 자넨 익살꾼이야. 광대 끼가 다분하다니까. 이보게, 우리가 구원받아야 할 대상이라고 했나? <고도를 기다리는 두 사람>! 그럴듯하지 않나?

리처드 난데없이 웬 고도요? 고도를 기다리는 자가 아직도 있소?

맥베스 고도를 기다리며 평생 길바닥에 서 있는 게 우리의 고달픈

everywhere. You can change your name but not your image.

Richard I sadly agree. Once it's stuck it's difficult to remove it. Shakespeare's portrayal of me will last forever, I have no doubt, and who shall blame him?

Macbeth What's the title of the play?

Richard Oh yes, I forgot to mention that important point. Since it's about us, they suggested that we choose the title. What shall it be?

Macbeth I leave it to you.

Richard No no! You're the one with more experience, so it's better that you should decide.

Macbeth What has experience to do with it?

Richard This is our first appearance in Korea, so it's better it comes from someone of your stature. You who might one day be Christopher Marlowe Macbeth's father, and that carries weight.

Macbeth You're a clown, full of tom-foolery. Listen, what about this? We are two people in need of salvation. "Two Men Waiting for Godot". How does that sound?

Richard Why suddenly bring Godot into this? Is someone still waiting for Godot?

Macbeth Isn't it our poor lot to stand in the street waiting

인생 아닌가? 고도를 희망의 하나님이라고 생각하면 되지. 우리 두 사람 모두 구원받을 처지라면서?

리처드 고도가 하나님이라는 증거가 있소?

맥베스 자네는 하늘나라를 바라본다고 하지 않았나?

리처드 작가 자신도 누군지 모른다는 그 고도가 나타날 리 있겠소? 그리고, 형님, 우리 제목은 셰익스피어와 관계가 있어야 하지 않겠습니까?

맥베스 우리가 셰익스피어 안에서 놀아야 한다고 했나? 그렇다면, <셰익스피어의 그림자>. 그러면 되겠군그래.

리처드 그거 좋습니다. <셰익스피어의 그림자> 광땡이오! 역시 관록을 무시할 수 없군요. 제목도 정해졌겠다, 이제 고만 일어나실까요?

맥베스 기다려주는 사람도 없는데 왜 그리 서둘러?

리처드 붕어들 밥 줘야 하오. 아픈 붕어 약도 먹여야 하고요.

맥베스 아스클레피오스 나셨네! 미물을 살뜰히 돌보는 걸 보니, 자네 가슴에 따듯한 구석이 있기는 있군. 그런 자가 사람을 왜 그리 해쳤던고?

리처드 철이 늦게 났소이다. 형님, 우리 두 사람 대화 듣는 거, 청중이 이제 지루해 할 거요. 이쯤에서 놓아줍시다.

forever for Godot? I look on Godot as God of hope. We're both in need of salvation, aren't we?

Richard Do you have proof that Godot is God?

Macbeth You were the one looking up to Heaven.

Richard Even the author doesn't know who Godot is, so it's not likely Godot will turn up here. But Macbeth, I really think our title has to have something to do with Shakespeare.

Macbeth Oh, Shakespeare! to do with Shakespeare! Well, what about "Shakespeare's Shadow"? That sounds good to me.

Richard "Shakespeare's Shadow"! Perfect! Experience pays. Well, now that we've got the title sorted out, let's go home.

Macbeth Why be in such a hurry to go when there's no one expecting you at home?

Richard I have to go and feed my goldfish. And give the sick one its medication.

Macbeth Behold Aesculapius! There must be a warm heart in you after all to see you taking care of such small creatures. And you, who caused all that devastation.

Richard I came to my senses rather late in life. The audience must be bored to death hearing us talk. It's time to let them go.

맥베스 나 청중 붙잡은 적 없네. 청중이 날 붙잡았지.

리처드 하! 형님 유머 감각이 눈부시게 늘고 있소.

맥베스 그래, 집에서는 고작 붕어하고 노는 거야? 언제부터 물고기에 관심이 생겼나?

리처드 형님, 헤어지기 심히 섭섭한 모양이시구려. 물고기는 로잘라인에게 분양받았다오. 고것들 노는 거 보고 있으면 나도 함께 헤엄치고 싶다니까요.

맥베스 로잘라인? 자네, <사랑의 헛수고>에 등장하는 프랑스 왕녀의 시녀를 말하는 건가?

리처드 그 로잘라인이 아니고요. 로미오가 실연당한 로잘라인이오. 우연히 만났는데 붕어가 새끼를 많이 낳았다고 분양할 사람을 찾더라고요.

맥베스 사람들이 자네 그림자만 보고도 도망간다더니, 그게 아니네. 여전히 악당의 매력을 발산하고 다니는 모양이군. 자네 발이 넓기는 넓구먼. 줄리엣은 그럼 로미오의 첫사랑이 아니었단 말인가?

리처드 로미오가 줄리엣 만나기 전에 사랑하던 애가 있었소. 형님은 기억나지 않을 거요. 그 애는 대사도 없고 무대에 등장하지 않거든요.

맥베스 로미오, 그 녀석 엉큼하네.

리처드 별걸 다 엉큼하다 하시네. 로미오가 실연당했다오. 얼마나

Macbeth My dear Richard. I have never kept them. They always keep me from going.

Richard I see that your sense of humour is improving.

Macbeth So you play with goldfish at home? Since when?

Richard I can see that you're loathe to part. The goldfish are given to me by Rosaline. When I see them swimming about, I want to join them.

Macbeth Rosaline, the lady-in-waiting of the Princess of France in *Love's Labour's Lost*?

Richard No, no, not that witty Rosaline but the Rosaline that Romeo loved in vain. I met her by chance, and her goldfish had spawned, and she was looking for someone to give away the little ones.

Macbeth You say people run a mile at the sight of your shadow, but I see that it's not the case. Villainy has its own attractions, and you're putting them to full use. You seem to know everyone. So Juliet wasn't Romeo's first love?

Richard No, there was someone before Romeo met Juliet. Romeo's Rosaline has no line in the play and she doesn't appear, so you must have forgotten her.

Macbeth Ah, he's a deep one.

Richard No, no, not his fault. He was rejected. He must have

마음이 허전하고 쓸쓸했겠소. 차가운 가슴을 녹여줄 상대가 필요한 그 시점에 줄리엣을 보고 한눈에 홀딱 간 거지요.

맥베스 자네가 직접 경험한 것처럼 들린다.

리처드 형님, 내가 사랑에 거리를 두는 건 말이오. 나도 터치스톤, 그 촌놈 말에 동감이라오. "사람들은 다 죽게 마련인지라 연애하는 자들도 바보짓 하다 무상하게 죽는 것이다." 그 광대 녀석 말이 그럴듯하게 들리오.

맥베스 여보게, 그건 터치스톤의 말이 아니고 로잘린드가 올란도에게 하는 말일세. "예부터 남자들이 죽어서 구더기의 밥이 되어왔지만 사랑 때문에 죽은 사나이는 한 명도 없다." 이 말을 한 거지.

리처드 우리 형님께서는 셰익스피어 대사를 모조리 꿰고 계시니, 놀랍소!

맥베스 과장이 심하네, 리처드. 어쨌거나 터치스톤 그자는 그래도 오드리와 결혼했잖은가?

리처드 그렇지요. 그를 오드리와 결혼시킨 므슈 멜랑콜리, 제이퀴즈 나리의 역할이 신통방통합니다. 자, 그럼 이제 고만 일어나실까요?

맥베스 이보게, 나도 제이퀴즈 역할을 자네한테 주고 싶네. 난 자네의 그 까칠한 자존심 따위는 버리고, 목숨 걸고 사랑할

felt lost and unhappy, and desperately needed someone to comfort him, and that was when Juliet appeared, and he just fell for her.

Macbeth You sound as if you've experienced that sort of thing yourself.

Richard The reason why I keep myself away from such affairs is the same as that rustic Touchstone's. He says something like it's the fate of everything in nature to die one day, but lovers foolishly believe in love, though they will meet the same fate. That's what the Fool thinks, and I agree with him.

Macbeth Touchstone never said that. It's Rosalind who said to Orlando: "Men have died from time to time and worms have eaten them, but not for love", she said that.

Richard You seem to know every line from Shakespeare. It's amazing.

Macbeth You exaggerate, Richard. Anyway, Touchstone ended up marrying Audrey, didn't he?

Richard Oh yes. Monsieur Melancholy Jacques did a good job there in bringing them together. Shall we get up and go now?

Macbeth I want to be a Jacques to you. I wish you would get rid of that fastidious pride of yours and meet a

여인을 만났으면 하네. 동방에서 올 때는 혼자 오지 말고 헬렌과 같은 지상 절세의 미녀와 함께 오게나!

리처드 아이고, 형님 농담 실력이 일취월장이오! 난 마법사가 아니올시다. 트로이 대신 무너트릴 도시도 없고요. 그리고 난 불나방처럼 뛰어드는 십 대 로미오도 아니고, 그렇다고, 군신 마르스와 비너스처럼 천상의 경지에 이르는, 그런 사랑에 목숨 버리는 안토니 장군도 못 되오. 아시겠소? 그러니, 겁나는 헬렌은 리스트에서 빼고, 올 때는 그 대신 형님 좋아하는 음악, 임윤찬 앨범을 갖고 오리다.

맥베스 그거 고맙네. 여보게, 내가 임윤찬 얘기를 자네한테 안 하고 헤어질 수야 없지. 내가 얼마 전에 그 천재 소년의 연주를 들으러 위그모어홀에 가지 않았겠나? 그때 생각하면 아직도 내 가슴이 덜덜 떨린다니까.

리처드 그렇게도 감동적이었소?

맥베스 아름다움과 경이로움의 극치였네. 터치 하나하나가 눈에 몽롱하게 들어오는 구슬 같았어. 돌담 사이를 두고 티스비를 기다리던 피라머스가, "아, 티스비의 목소리를 보는구나" 하는 그 대사가 번쩍 떠오른 거야.

리처드 소리를 본다는 형님의 비유, 아주 멋지십니다.

맥베스 파우스트의 대사 한 줄이 자네 뒤통수를 때렸다더니, 나야말로 피라머스의 별것 아닌 그 한마디가 내 정수리를 때리

woman you would give your life for. When you return from the East, don't come back alone but bring a world-class beauty like Helen.

Richard You must be joking. I'm not a magician, and there's no Troy to sack. Nor am I a reckless teenager like Romeo. Nor could I ever be like Anthony with his Cleopatra, veritable Mars and Venus, those two. I'll leave Helen behind and bring back for you some music you would like, Yunchan Lim's latest album.

Macbeth Wow, that would be sooo great! Thank you Richard! Now that you mention him, I can't leave you without saying a word or two about Yunchan Lim. Some time ago, I went to hear that genius play in Wigmore Hall. My heart still beats at the memory of it.

Richard Was it that good?

Macbeth It was the pinnacle of beauty and wonder. Each key he touched was like a shining pearl drop before your eyes. What Pyramus said before the wall as he was waiting for Thisbe suddenly lept to my mind: "I see a voice".

Richard Ah, seeing a voice is a good image.

Macbeth You mentioned how a line from Faustus threw you. Well, those few words of Pyramus's knocked me out.

더라고! 또 하나, 캘리밴의 대사도 내 머리를 흔들었어. "구름이 열리면서 하늘의 보물들이 한눈에 들어와요. 꿈속의 보물들은 마치 내 머리 위로 쏟아져 내릴 듯 보이지요. 그러다 깨어나면 난 다시 꿈을 꾸고 싶어 운답니다." 내가 느끼는 임윤찬의 연주를 캘리밴이 그대로 표현해 주었네. 나도 울고 싶더라니까.

리처드 그 비유 정말 비상합니다. 형님은 셰익스피어의 그림자 안에서 확실히 놀고 계시네요. 그 안에서는 우는 꿈도 꾸시는구려! 울고 싶을 때는, 꿈만 꾸지 마시고, 마음껏 우시오. 형님, 눈물샘도 훈련이 필요하다오. 막히면 큰일이오.

맥베스 『태풍』에서 가장 주옥같은 대사를 셰익스피어가 그 음탕한 괴물에게 허용했다는 게 인상적이야.

리처드 캘리밴이 그 섬과 밀접한 관계가 있다는 의미지요.

맥베스 내가 자네 덕분에 지구 돌아가는 소리 많이 듣고 간다. 코리아에 가면 셰익스피어 학회 분들께 축하 인사와 고맙다는 인사도 잘 전해 주게.

리처드 알겠습니다. 다녀와서 연락드리리다. 그런데, 형님, 이거 하나는 꼭 기억하시오! 관객은 우리 같은 악역을 증오하면서도 좋아하고 즐거워한다는 사실을 말이오! 안녕! (페이드아웃.)

Caliban's speech too had the same effect, let me tell you: "in dreaming,/ the Clouds me thought would open, and show riches/ Ready to drop upon me, that when I wak'd,/ I cried to dream again." These words express precisely what I felt about Yunchan Lim's performance. I wanted to cry when the concert was over.

Richard Wonderful imagery! There's no doubt that you are firmly ensconced in Shakespeare's shadow. Well, dream of weeping, and weep when you want to, Macbeth. Tear glands need to be put to use after all, and it would be disastrous to have them dried up.

Macbeth I find it odd that Shakespeare should have given such splendid lines to that lecherous monster Caliban in *The Tempest.*

Richard It's because he is part of the island.

Macbeth Thanks to you, I've learned a lot about what's going on in the world. When you go to Korea, please give the Association my felicitations and thanks.

Richard Of course. I'll be in touch when I'm back. And please remember this. The audience hate villains like us, but they also love us and enjoy seeing us on stage. (Fade out.)

[장면 3] 에필로그. 리처드와 오필리아의 대화.

(페이드인. 공원의 다른 장소. 같은 때. *오필리아가 호수 옆 벤치에 앉아 열심히 책을 읽고 있다. 반대쪽에서 리처드가 등장한다.*)

리처드 (*혼잣말로*) 오, 저기 저 아가씨는 오필리아가 아니냐? 여전히 아름다운 요정이로다! 갑자기 내 가슴이 왜 이렇게 떨리지? 저 여인이 내 심장에 불을 지피는구나. 나, 리처드 3세의 심장이 여자를 보고 이토록 요동친 적이 있었나? 이 무슨 징조냐? 그런데 어떻게 저 여자에게 다가서지? 뭐라고 말을 붙이지? 아무 말이나 그냥 던져 보라고? 모른 척하고 나를 쳐다볼 때까지 그녀 앞을 왔다 갔다 하라고? 그건 내가 미치지 않고서야 할 수 없는 짓이다. 그런데 내가 미치지 않은 것도 아니지 않은가? 사랑이란 사람을 미치게 하는 마술인가? 로미오도 안토니도 나무랄 수가 없구나.

[Scene 3] Epilogue. Richard and Ophelia talking.

(Fade in. *A different spot in the same place and time. Ophelia is sitting on a bench by the lake, absorbed in reading. Richard makes an appearance from the opposite side.*)

Richard (*Talking to himself*) Oh, there's Ophelia! A beautiful nymph, no less! Why is my heart suddenly pounding? She is the cause of it. Has my heart ever pounded at the sight of a woman? No! What does it mean? How shall I approach her? And what shall I say to her? Anything that comes into my head? Or just walk up and down before her as if I didn't notice her? No, that would drive me mad. But I think I am mad. Is love magic that turns you mad? Now I see what Romeo and Anthony went through! But their love was returned. Romeo danced with Juliet, and Anthony went boating with Cleopatra.

그렇지만 그들은 나처럼 혼자서 짝사랑한 게 아니었지. 한 쌍은 춤도 추고 또 한 쌍은 뱃놀이도 하며 서로 짝지어 놀지 않았느냐? 내가 저 여자 앞으로 다가간다 치고― 뭐라고 말을 건네야 하나? 독서에 여념 없는 저 여인을 보라! 오, 참으로 경건하고 아름다운 자태로다. 앤을 유혹하던 나의 옛날 뱃심은 어디로 사라졌느냐? 가짜 행동에는 선수이면서, 진짜에는 아마추어도 못 된단 말인가? 성령이여, 도우소서! 기적이 일어났습니다. 나의 님프가 바로 눈앞에 나타났습니다. 도와주소서! 예, 앞으로 가겠습니다. 전진합니다! (*그녀 앞으로 가까이 다가간다.*) 아름다운 님프시여! 안녕하십니까? 오필리아 아가씨 맞지요?

오필리아 (*깜짝 놀라면서*) 저 . . . 저를 아시나요?

리처드 아이고, 미안하오. 놀라서 책을 다 떨구시는구려! (*책을 집어서 돌려주며*) 자, 여기 책을 받으시지요. 아가씨를 해치려는 사람이 절대 아니니 안심하시오. 아가씨를 그렇게 놀래줄 만큼 내 인상이 험상궂소? 그대는 오필리아 아가씨가 맞지요?

오필리아 네, 오필리아 맞습니다.

리처드 십자가 목걸이를 보니, 수녀원에 계시오?

오필리아 아닙니다. 그냥 평신도입니다.

리처드 밑도 끝도 없는 외람된 질문이오만, 신앙생활이 만족스럽고 행복하오?

They both had a jolly time with their lovers. If I approach her, should I say something to her? Look at her absorbed in her book. Isn't it a bewitching sight? Where is the brazenness of Richard with Anne? I, who am so good at improvisation, is powerless before truth. Oh, Holy Spirit, help me! A miracle! I behold a nymph before my eyes! Help me to approach her. Yes, I am going towards her. (*Approaching*) Beauteous nymph, greetings! Are you Ophelia?

Ophelia (*Startled*) Do you know me?

Richard I'm so sorry. I surprised you, and you've dropped your book. (*picks up the book and gives it to her*) Don't worry. I'm not going to harm you. Do I look so fierce that you should look so scared? You're Ophelia, aren't you?

Ophelia Yes, I'm Ophelia.

Richard You're wearing a cross. Are you from a nunnery?

Ophelia No. I'm not a nun, though a believer.

Richard I know this is an odd question, but are you happy with your faith?

오필리아 네, 그래요. "내가 너희에게 주는 평안은 세상이 주는 평안과 다르다"라는 주님의 말씀이 영혼에 스며듭니다.

리처드 나도 그 비슷한 평안을 알고 있소. 그런데, 내 경우는 물속에서 경험한답니다.

오필리아 잠수부시군요.

리처드 잠수부요? 이렇게 생긴 몸도 잠수부가 될 수 있소? 그건 아니올시다.

오필리아 물속에서 평안을 느낀다고 하시니, 그런 생각이 들었어요. 선생님은 저를 알아보시는데, 선생님이 누구신지 여쭤봐도 실례가 되지 않겠지요? 선생님은 제가 매주 뵙고 있는 분이기는 합니다만.

리처드 나를 매주 본다고요? 어디서요?

오필리아 교회에서요. 항상 같은 구석 자리에 앉으시더군요. 그러다 예배가 끝나기도 전에 살그머니 빠져나가시는 모습을 매주 지켜보았어요. 왜 항상 그 구석 자리에 앉으시는지요?

리처드 그럼 우리가 주일마다 한 지붕 밑에서, 같은 예배당 안에 있었다는 겁니까? 이건 기적 같은 얘기요. 오! 놀라운 일이오. 내 이름은 리처드라 하오. 리처드 글로스터. 구체적으로 나를 밝히자면, 리처드 3세요.

오필리아 (*자리에서 벌떡 일어나며*) 아, 군주님이시군요! 군주님을 제가 감히 몰라 뵈었네요. 용서하세요.

Ophelia Yes. The Lord says, "Peace I leave with you, my peace I give unto you: not as the world giveth, give I unto you". These words fill my soul.

Richard I know something about that peace, but I experience it under water.

Ophelia You're a scuba-diver?

Richard A diver? No, no. Not in my physical condition.

Ophelia I thought you might be one as you said you find peace under water. You seem to know me, but if you don't mind, can I ask who you are? I know I've seen you every week.

Richard You've seen me every week? Where?

Ophelia In the church. You always sit at the back in the same corner. Then you always steal out before the service is over.

Richard Are you suggesting that we've been sitting under the same roof every Sunday, in the same church? It sounds like a miracle to me. My name is Richard, Richard of Gloucester. Richard III to be specific.

Ophelia (*Getting up*) Ah, Your Majesty, King Richard. I didn't recognize you. Please forgive me.

리처드 일어날 것 없어요. 어서 앉으시오. (*오필리아는 앉는다.*) 호칭은 무시하고, 그냥 리처드라고 불러 주면 고맙겠소.

오필리아 그건 무엄하지요. 감히 임금님 칭호를 빼고 부를 수 있나요?

리처드 내가 나라의 녹을 먹고 살고는 있지만, 지금 난 그대의 왕이 아니오. 그냥 리처드라고 편하게 불러 주면 고맙겠소, 오필리아 아가씨.

오필리아 네, 군주님. 정 그러시다면 그렇게 하지요. 리처드!

리처드 고맙소. 뭇사람들이 내 이름을 불렀지만, 그대가 나를 부르는 리처드 소리는 흡사 저기 떠 있는 무지개가 부르는 소리처럼 아름답게 들립니다. 오필리아는 님프가 맞는 모양이오. 내가 왜 항상 그 구석에 앉느냐고요? 나 자신을 숨기고 싶은 모양이오.

오필리아 제 눈에는 제일 먼저 눈에 띄는 자리인데요.

리처드 사람들 눈을 피해서 숨는다는 게 오히려 들키는 꼴이 되었구려. 님프 옆에 이 몸이 잠시 앉아도 되겠소?

오필리아 물론이지요. 여기 앉으세요. (*리처드는 앉는다.*) 군주님의 무지개 표현이 재미있네요, 오늘 보기 드물게 무지개가 떴어요. 좋은 징조여요.

리처드 내 이름을 한 번 더 불러 주겠소?

오필리아 네-? 아, 물론이지요. 리처드?

Richard No, no, don't get up. Please sit down. (*Ophelia sits down.*) Just ignore my title and call me Richard, thanks.

Ophelia That would be improper. How could I leave out your title?

Richard I may be on the country's payroll, but I'm not your king any longer. Don't stand on ceremony and just call me Richard, Ophelia.

Ophelia Well, if that's your wish, I will, Richard.

Richard Thank you! Many people have uttered my name, but from your lips Richard sounds as beautiful as the rainbow over there. You must be a true nymph. Why do I always sit in a corner? Perhaps I want to hide.

Ophelia But to me, it's the most visible place.

Richard I see that I've chosen a wrong place to sit. May I sit down?

Ophelia Of course. Please. (*Richard sits.*) Your mentioning the rainbow is curious. You don't see a rainbow everyday, but there it is today. It's a good omen.

Richard If you don't mind, can you please say my name once more?

Ophelia Oh . . . of course, Richard.

리처드 고맙소. 그 악명 높은 이름 석 자가 내 귀에 이렇게 달콤하게 들릴 때도 있다니! 놀랍구려. 오필리아 아가씨 덕분에 나도 내 이름을 이제부터는 아껴줘야 할 것 같소. 이 공원에는 자주 나오시오?

오필리아 네. 여기서 책 읽으면서 백조들 떠도는 모습도 구경하고 있노라면 편안해요. 한적하고 차분한 분위기여서 독서하기에 아주 좋은 곳이어요.

리처드 내가 그렇다면 방해꾼이 되었나 보구려.

오필리아 아닙니다. 전혀 그렇지 않습니다.

리처드 아름다운 님프! 그대는 기도문을 읽고 있었소?

오필리아 군주님— 아니, 리처드, 전 님프가 아니어요. '님프' 빼고 편하게 그냥 오필리아라고 불러 주세요. 그리고 이 책은 시집이어요. 어떤 의미로는 시도 기도문과 같다고 할 수 있지요.

리처드 아— 시를 좋아하시는 님프! 내가 고백 하나 해도 되겠소? 이곳에서 그대를 발견하자마자 나보다 내 가슴이 먼저 우당탕 뛰는 거였소. 워즈워스의 시 가운데, 어른이 되고 늙어도 무지개를 보면 어린 시절처럼 가슴이 뛰기를 소망한다는 시가 있지요? 뛰는 가슴이 멈추면 차라리 죽는 게 낫다고 시인이 썼어요. 표현이 좀 과격하다고 생각했는데, 지금 내 심정이 바로 그런 상태라오.

Richard Thank you. That my infamous name should sound so sweet! Thanks to you. I feel I shouldn't defame my name so much now. Do you come here often?

Ophelia Oh, yes. I read and watch the swans, and I feel at peace. This is a quiet spot, so it's very good for reading.

Richard I must be disturbing you!

Ophelia Not at all.

Richard Beautiful nymph, are you reading a prayer book?

Ophelia Your Majesty, no Richard. I'm not a nymph. Please leave out the nymph bit and simply call me Ophelia. This is a book of poetry. Though in some sense poems are prayers.

Richard Ah, a nymph who loves poetry! Can I confess something? When I saw you, my heart started to beat. Didn't poet Wordsworth write something about a grown man's heart leaping at the sight of a rainbow as it did when a child? He wrote that it would be better to die than no longer have your heart leaping at anything. The expression is a bit exaggerated, but that's what I feel at the moment.

오필리아 무지개는 노아에게 징표로 보여 주신 하나님의 언약이어요. 그 약속을 기억하고 감사하며 경건하게 살라는 메시지를 담고 있지요.

리처드 아, 그런 뜻으로 쓰인 표현이었군요. 기독교 국가에서 왕 노릇까지 한 나의 무지함을 용서해주시오.

오필리아 군주님께서 무슨 그런 말씀을! "나의 하루하루 날들이 경건에 매이기를 바란다"라는 그 시의 마지막 두 줄이 제 마음을 붙들어 줍니다.

리처드 그대의 말대로 그 시는 진정한 기도문이로구려. 하나 물어봐도 되겠소? 너무 개인적인 질문이라고 생각하면 대답하지 않아도 좋소.

오필리아 혹시, 햄릿 왕자에 관한 건가요?

리처드 역시 영리한 님프라서 눈치가 빠르시군요. 지금도 만나는 사이요?

오필리아 그분은 수도원에서 생활한다는 소문만 들었을 뿐, 잘 모릅니다.

리처드 그대 보고 "수녀원으로 가라!"고 등 떠밀고 소리소리 지르던 자가 본인이 간 모양이구려.

오필리아 햄릿 왕자님과 저와의 관계는 제 부친 때문에 문제가 좀 불거졌어요. 아버지는 왕자님의 광기를 저에 대한 짝사랑 때문이라고 확신했으니까요.

Ophelia The rainbow is a sign God gave to Noah to remember his covenant and live piously.

Richard Oh, I see. I didn't know that, and I, once the king of a Christendom. Please forgive my ignorance.

Ophelia Oh no, there's no need to apologize. "And I could wish my days to be/ Bound each to each by natural piety", the last two lines of the poem. They are very moving.

Richard As you say, this poem is a true prayer. Can I ask you a question? If you think it's too personal, you don't have to answer me.

Ophelia Does it, by any chance, concern Prince Hamlet?

Richard You're an astute nymph to guess that. Do you still see him?

Ophelia I heard that he's living in some monastery, but I know nothing more of him.

Richard He told you to go to a nunnery, but it seems that he's gone to one himself.

Ophelia My relationship with the prince became openly known because of my father. My father thought he had gone mad because of his love for me.

리처드 아가씨도 그렇게 믿었소?

오필리아 처음에는 그런 줄 알았는데, 이야기가 전혀 달랐어요. 남자들은 자기들 마음이 뒤틀리면 왜 애인이나 아내를 창녀 취급하는지 모르겠어요. 실은 저를 창녀 취급하고 몰아붙인 그 점이 저를 정말로 미치게 했으니까요. 오셀로 장군도 아내를 의심하면서, 그 순결한 여인을 "창녀"라고 부르고 목 졸라 죽였잖아요. 리온티즈도 아내 허마이오니를 의심하고 아내를 독살하려 했었고요. 사람이 미쳐도 그렇게 미치면 안 되는 거 아니어요?

리처드 햄릿이 당신을 의심했소?

오필리아 그건 아니었어요. 그분은 자기 분풀이를 저에게 터트렸을 뿐이어요. 제가 희생 제물이 된 셈인데, 저를 여성 전체의 상징으로 삼고 증오한 거겠지요.

리처드 그 사람이 왜 그랬다고 생각하시오?

오필리아 선왕 햄릿이 갑자기 죽고, 왕비 거트루드는 시동생 클로디어스와 곧바로 결혼했으니— 어머니와 각별한 사이인 아들 눈에는 결혼식이 장례식으로 보였을 겁니다.

리처드 프로이트가 말하는 소위 오이디푸스 콤플렉스라는 거군요. 그런 점도 있을 수 있겠소만. 그래도 난 이자가 못마땅하오. 그대의 옛 남친을 비난조로 말하는 게 듣기 거북하겠구려. 내가 치졸해 보일 것이오만. 좀 떠들어도 되겠소?

Richard Do you believe that yourself?

Ophelia I had thought so at first, but realized there was a completely different explanation. I don't know why men, when they get all mixed up inside, start treating their lovers or wives as sluts. In truth, it was his treating me like a slut that turned me insane. Othello suspected his wife and called that pure woman a strumpet, and strangled her to death. Leontes doubted his wife Hermione and tried to poison her. That's madness. They shouldn't misbehave like that.

Richard Did Hamlet doubt you?

Ophelia No, he didn't. He just took out everything, all his anger, on me. I was the scapegoat. He saw me as representing all women, and he hated me.

Richard Why did he?

Ophelia His father, the king suddenly died, and Queen Gertrude married his brother immediately. Hamlet was very close to his mother, so it must have been a shock. No wonder the wedding looked like a funeral to him.

Richard It's what Freud calls Oedipus complex. I suppose it's possible to look at it like that, but I don't like him. I must be offending you to disparage your old boyfriend, and I must look a mean sort of fellow to you. But can I talk on a bit?

오필리아 세상에 완벽한 사람이 어디 있겠어요? 그분의 어떤 점이 귀하에게 거슬렸는지 들어보고 싶습니다.

리처드 너그러운 님프시여, 고맙소. 나도 햄릿 왕자의 고귀함을 알고 있소. 나 같은 자와는 하늘과 땅 차이요. 고상한 인물임에는 틀림이 없소. 그러나 사랑하는 여자에게 그렇게 상처 주는 독한 말을 쏟아 내는 건 나로선 이해가 안 되오. 용납이 안 됩니다. 연인 관계의 아가씨를 몰아붙이는 태도도 그렇고, 삼촌과 재혼한 모친을 침실에서 닦달하는 모습, 끔찍하오. 참고 봐주기 힘든 모습이오. 그래서 볼테르는 셰익스피어를 "술 취한 야만인"이라고 헐뜯은 모양이오. 프랑스인들은 어쨌거나 좀 까칠한 구석이 있다 치고. 프랑스 신고전주의자들은 시간, 장소, 행동의 삼 일치를 극구성의 필수로 인식했소. 그런데 호머나 셰익스피어 같은 천부적인 천재는 이들이 주장하는 적절성과 규칙에 얽매일 필요가 없는 희귀한 존재임을 알아보지 못한 것이오.

오필리아 군주님도 극을 쓰시면 재미있게 잘 쓰실 것 같아요.

리처드 허허, 어디서 한 번쯤 들어본 소리요. 그러나 그건 전혀 아니올시다. 아가씨는 내가 비난하던 햄릿 얘기나 마저 들어주시구려. "돼지우리 침대에서 부둥켜안고 땀범벅으로 뒹굴지 말라"고 어머니를 훈시하는 이 아들의 태도가 거북하지 않소? 어머니가 흡사 몸을 파는 창기라도 되는 듯

Ophelia Oh, yes. I believe nobody is perfect. I want to hear why you don't like Hamlet.

Richard Generous nymph, thanks! I know that Hamlet is a worthy young man, so different from me. He is, without doubt, a noble young man. But I can't understand him pouring out those harsh words to hurt a woman he loves. His harsh behaviour to you and venomous words to his mother in her bed chamber – those are terrible scenes, hard to watch. That's probably why Voltaire called Shakespeare a "drunken savage". The French are of course a bit more restrained in their tragedies. Their neo-classicists insist that the three unities of place, time and action are essential in a play. They didn't recognize the fact that geniuses like Homer and Shakespeare didn't need to follow such things as decorum and rules.

Ophelia I think you would make a good playwright.

Richard Oh, someone else said that before. But no, I don't think I would. Let's get back to Hamlet, and let me tell you the rest. "Stew'd in corruption, honeying and making love/ Over the nasty sty." Terrible words to utter. Don't you find these words a bit too harsh? How could he treat his mother like a common whore!

무자비하게 다루는 그런 장면을 그대는 이해할 수 있소? 난 내 혀를 깨물면 깨물었지, 사랑하는 여인에게, 더군다나 모자 관계가 각별한 마마보이 아들이 그토록 표독스럽게 모친을 몰아붙일 수 있는지. 상상할 수 없소.

오필리아 사랑에 눈이 멀면 무슨 짓이든 할 수 있으니, "사랑은 눈먼 봉사라 연인들의 눈엔 자신들이 저지르는 어리석은 모습이 보이지 않는다"라고 제시카가 말하더군요.

리처드 테세우스도 광인이나 연인, 시인들을 모두 상상력으로 차 있는 똑같은 자들로 보았소. 난 사랑을 조롱할 생각은 조금도 없소. 사랑보다 더 값진 감정이 하늘 아래 어디 있겠소? 신자나 불신자나 결혼식에서 주례자가 신랑 신부 세워놓고 애용하는 문구가 바로 고린도 전서 13장의 사랑 구절 아니오? 그렇지만 부모든 애인이든, 진실로 사랑한다면 이들의 가슴에 비수를 꽂는 살인적인 폭언을 어찌할 수 있겠소? 사랑은 아무리 추상적 개념이라 해도 존중해야 하는, 마땅히 존중받아야 하는, 숭고한 존엄, 그게 바로 사랑이라고 생각하오. 내 정의는 그렇소. 그래서 사람들이 안타깝게 한숨짓는 트로일러스와 크레시다의 금이 간 사랑을 난 조금도 동정하지 않는다오.

오필리아 트로이의 전쟁 상황에서 어쩔 수 없이 깨진 이들의 불행한 사랑을 관객은 가엾게 여기고 있지요.

I would bite my tongue out before I could say such things. And I thought he was his mother's darling, which makes his behaviour doubly hard to imagine.

Ophelia But love makes you blind and can drive you to do strange things. "Love is blind, and lovers cannot see/ The pretty follies that themselves commit", so Jessica said.

Richard "The lunatic, the lover, and the poet/ Are of imagination all compact", so Theseus said. I have no intention of making fun of love. What could be more precious than love? Whether you are a believer or not, at weddings the sermon is always about love as defined in the first Corinthians 13. But if you really loved your parents or lover, really loved them, it's not possible to utter murderous words that will be daggers to them. You must hold love as something precious, however abstract it seems. It's something sacred and holy, don't you think? That's my definition of love. That's why I have no sympathy for Troilus and Cressida, though many pity them.

Ophelia Well, their love failed because of the war, and the audience feel that it's not entirely their fault.

리처드 그렇다 해도 이들의 사랑과 성(性)에 대한 냉소적인 표현은 당혹스럽구려. 더구나 트로일러스의 태도는 메스껍소. 이자는 크레시다에 대한 이상적 이미지가 깨지자, 사랑의 성관계를 먹고 버린 음식에 비유하고 있단 말이오. 사랑의 행위를 부패의 상징으로 삼고 음식의 배설물로 보다니, 괴기스럽구려. 여인을 혐오하는 그의 태도는 햄릿과 비슷하오. 이들은 낭만적인 사랑이 불가능한 자들이오. 크레시다의 모델은 트로이의 파리스 왕자가 납치한 헬렌이 아니겠소?

오필리아 군주님은 어떤 사랑을 이상적으로 여기시는지요?

리처드 비 온 후 나뭇가지 사이로 비치는 맑은 햇살 같은, 청초한 로미오와 줄리엣의 사랑. 이게 나의 이상형이오.

오필리아 크레시다와 트로일러스도 누구 못지않게 서로 사랑하기는 했지요.

리처드 그건 그렇지 않소. 처음부터 이들의 태도는 순수하지도 순진하지도 않았소. 서로 끌리면 당당하게 나설 일이지, 왜 두 사람 사이에 뚜쟁이를 끌어들입니까? 크레시다는 처음 등장할 때부터 "원하는 여자를 얻고 나면 열정이 식으니, 주기 전까지는 죽도록 매달리게 해라." 이따위 소리를, 그것도 애교라고 하고 있소이다. 일단 잡힌 물고기는 사내들이 거들떠보지 않는다는, 추잡한 부정적인 사고를 사랑의

Richard I find the cynical way they talk about love unacceptable, and Troilus's behaviour is vile. When he found that Cressida no longer lived up to his ideal, he begins to talk of love and sex as scraps of food. He looks on sexual love as a symbol of corruption, as excrement, and that's disgusting. I find there's something similar in his and Hamlet's misogyny. Both are incapable of true romantic love. Cressida's is a second Helen to him.

Ophelia What kind of love seems ideal to you then?

Richard The pure love of Romeo and Juliet, which is like a ray of sunlight shining through wet branches after a rainfall. That's my ideal.

Ophelia But Troilus and Cressida did love each other truly, I think.

Richard You're wrong there. Even from the beginning, their love was neither pure nor innocent. If they really loved each other, why didn't they just get on with it rather than bring in a go-between? Cressida takes as maxim of love something like this: "Achievement is command; ungain'd beseech." She thought it was clever to think that men lose interest once the fish is caught. That's what she thinks love is all about. A woman who gives you a slap in the face before your

정석으로 가슴에 새기는 이 여자, 크레시다. 징그럽지 않소? 시작도 하기 전에 배신을 품고 있는 멍때리는 여자요. 줄리엣 입에서는 절대로 나올 수 없는, 상상도 할 수 없는 소리 아니오? 교활한 율리시스의 표현대로, 크레시다는 기회만 있으면, "아무 때나 건드릴 수 있는 음탕한 창녀"와 다를 바 없는 여자요. 이들은 사랑을 덫에 걸린 형태로 인식하고 있소. 난 판다로스나 터사이테스같이 사랑을 싸구려 짝퉁 상품으로 팔아먹는 인간 말종들을 경멸하오.

오필리아 군주님의 말씀에 저도 동감합니다. 저 역시 로미오와 줄리엣의 사랑을 보석처럼 빛나는 한줄기 수정체와 같다고 생각합니다. 그래서 로미오와 줄리엣이라는 이름이 사랑의 상징적 주인공으로 전 세계 만인의 가슴에 새겨져 있는 거 아니겠어요?

리처드 오필리아 아가씨, 그대와 나는 바라보는 방향이 같은 것 같소. 내 마음에 안 드는 햄릿의 또 다른 태도 하나를 지적해 볼까요? 듣기 거북하다면 말하지 않으리다.

오필리아 아닙니다. 군주님께서는 제가 공감하는 부분을 많이 말씀해주고 계십니다.

리처드 "디도와 이니어스"의 극을 대하면서 햄릿이 배우들에게 뭐라고 하던가요? "내 기억으로 이 극은 대중 취향에 맞지 않았네. 돼지 목에 진주 목걸이였지." 값어치를 모르는

relationship even begins. Don't you find that disgusting? Juliet would have been incapable of uttering such words. According to wily Ulysses, Cressida is "one of the sluttish spoils of opportunity/ And daughter of the game". They regard love as fishing and being caught in a net. I hate and despise the dregs of humanity like Pandarus and Thersites, who treat love like some cheap fake good and trade in it.

Ophelia I agree with you, and I too think of Romeo and Juliet's love as shining crystal of a jewel. Isn't that why their love is engraved in everyone's heart as the emblem of true love?

Richard Dear Ophelia, I think we too think alike on this. Shall I tell you another thing I dislike about Hamlet? But I won't if you don't want to hear.

Ophelia Oh, no. I find we agree on many things.

Richard Concerning the play *Dido and Aeneas,* do you remember what Hamlet said to the actors? "the play, I remember, pleased not the million, 'twas caviare to the general." He meant it has no meaning to those

자들에게는 소용없다는, 평범한 대중을 무시하는 이 말투는 그의 교만이 그대로 묻어난 것이오. 내가 좀 예민한지는 모르겠소만, 이거야말로 햄릿의 속물근성을 드러낸 것 아니겠소? 난 속으로, "그래, 너 자-알 났다, 자-알 났어! 짜아-식!" 나의 억하심정에서 나오는 비방이 아니라, 어디까지나 내 속에서 우러나는 순수한 반응이오.

오필리아 그분은 인정도 많은 분이어요.

리처드 마음이 넓다는 말로 들리오. 옛 애인을 옹호해 주고 싶은 심정은 이해합니다. 그렇소. 그자의 좋은 점은 좋은 점이고, 그러나 내 비위에 맞지 않은, 싫은 건 싫은 거니까. 3막 2장에서 어머니한테 불려 가는 길에, 고도의 냉혹성을 보여 주는, 짧지만 인상적인 독백을 그가 토로합니다. 어머니에 대한 증오심을 스스로 진정시키는 장면이오. "제발 천륜의 정은 잊지 말자. 잔인한 네로의 영혼이 내 가슴 속에 들어오지 않게 하자. 가혹하게는 대할지라도 천륜의 정은 저버리지 말자. 직접 단도로 찔러서는 안 된다. 날카로운 언사의 비수를 어머니 가슴에 꽂자." 네로가 어머니 아그리피나를 죽인 것처럼 그 역시 어머니를 죽이고 싶은, 죽일 것 같은 증오심을 뿜어내고 있는 거요. 육신은 죽이지 말고. 말로, 혀로, 독설로 어머니의 가슴을 도려내겠다는, 그의 형이상학적, 가학적 살인 의도에 소름이 끼칩니다.

who couldn't value it as they should. It showed he despised the common audience, an instance of sheer arrogance. I may be over-reacting, but I thought it showed his snobbery. I said to myself, so you think you're so great, so different from the rest of us, ha! I don't say this lightly. I really mean it.

Ophelia There is a sweet side to him, you know.

Richard This shows your generous nature. I perfectly understand your desire to defend your old boyfriend. I know he has some good qualities, but what I dislike, I dislike for a reason. In Act 3:2 he's on his way to see his mother, and he utters a short but really cruel soliloquy. "O heart, lose not thy nature; let not ever/ The soul of Nero enter thy firm bosom/ Let me be cruel, not unnatural:/ I will speak daggers to her, but use none." He's trying to suppress his hatred, but just as Nero killed his mother Agrippina, so Hamlet is spewing out his murderous feelings for his mother not to kill her bodily, but to stab her heart with his tongue, a metaphysically sadistic act. It gives me the shivers.

나로 말하면, 사람 목숨을 많이 해친 흉측한 죄인이오만, 사랑하는 사람의 얼굴에 대고 햄릿처럼 그렇게 몰인정한 짓은 하지 못하오. 필경은 내가 먼저 울어버릴 것이오.

오필리아 그렇다면, 군주님은 진정으로 사랑해 본 여인이 있었나요?

리처드 아가씨, 그에 대한 내 대답은 아껴두겠소. 그러면, 오필리아 아가씨, 그대는 햄릿 말고 진정 사랑한 남자가 있었소?

오필리아 저도 거기에 대한 대답은 아껴두겠습니다, 전하.

리처드 하하하— 그대와 나, 우리 두 사람은 의외로 언어가 잘 통하는구려. 비어트리스와 베네디크가 보여주는, 서로 끔찍이 끌리면서도 안 그런 척 감정을 숨기는, 그런 "즐거운 전쟁"이 없어도 우리 둘 사이에는 공통분모가 많이 있겠소이다.

오필리아 군주님, 저는 있는 그대로 표현하는 것 이상으로 달리 말을 돌리는 재주는 없습니다.

리처드 어쨌든 햄릿 얘기는 내 입에서 더 험한 말이 나오지 않도록 여기서 그치겠소. 죄 많은 이 몸이야말로 한없이 거듭나야 할 사람이라오. 용서하시오. 그대 옆에 앉아 있는 내 모습은 흡사 "미녀와 야수"의 형상을 연상시키지는 않는지 모르겠소.

오필리아 군주님! 군주님은 소설도 쓰시겠어요. 정말 엉뚱한 말씀을 하시네요. 사랑에 대한 말씀을 들으면서, 사람마다 성격도

I know I am a brutal man who killed many, but I don't think I can utter such cruel words to the loved ones, and to their face too as Hamlet had done. I would break down and weep, I'm sure.

Ophelia Have you ever loved a woman truly?

Richard Dear Ophelia, I'll leave that unanswered. But you, have you ever loved a man other than Hamlet?

Ophelia I too will leave that unanswered, Richard.

Richard Ha, ha, ha. You and I, we seem to understand each other pretty well. Without that "merry war" Beatrice and Benedick fought when they pretended to be indifferent when they, in fact, were very much in love. I think you and I have much in common, though we don't fight like them.

Ophelia I say what I feel, and am no good at pretending.

Richard Well, I'll stop talking about Hamlet before I say anything more disparaging. I am a sinner and need much reformation, so please forgive me. My sitting next to you must conjure up the image of the Beauty and the Beast.

Ophelia Oh no, Richard, not at all. I think you would make a good novelist too. Hearing you talk about love

생각도 다르니, 서로의 정서적 언어가 다르면 교감이 어렵겠다는 생각이 들었습니다. 그러나 순수한 사랑을 욕보이는 행동은 모욕감을 느끼기 이전에 가슴 저미는 슬픈 일이지요. 저도 사랑에 대한 부정적인 자세를 배척합니다. 성경에 보면, 배다른 여동생 다말을 흠모한 나머지, 죽겠다며 신음하고 앓던 암논이 소녀를 완력으로 능욕하고 나서는, 미움이 전의 사랑보다 더 커져서 문밖으로 끌어내고 문빗장을 지르는 장면이 있거든요. 이런 행동은 이해가 안 됩니다. 그런데 이런 게 모두 인간 심리의 신비한 수수께끼 아니겠어요? 햄릿 왕자의 가려진 심장을 들여다볼 수 없는 것처럼 말이어요.

리처드 사랑하는 사람끼리 서로 백년해로를 약속했다 해도, 뜻하지 않은 상황으로 변심할 수도 있겠지요. 난 내가 정신과 의사가 아니니, 진단을 내릴 수는 없지만, 암논의 경우는 지극히 병적인, 이상 심리로 보이는구려. 오필리아 아가씨, 그대에게 용기를 내어 감히 묻고 싶은 게 있소. 햄릿 왕자와 헤어진 진정한 동기가 무엇이었는지 말해줄 수 있겠소?

오필리아 우리가 갈라지게 된 발단은 아버지에 대한 저의 절대 순종 때문이었어요. 저와 햄릿 사이의 대화를 왕이 몰래 엿들을 수 있도록 저의 선친께서 연출을 꾸미셨어요. 저를 햄릿의 먹잇감으로 풀어놓은 셈인데, 영리한 왕자님이 그 함정에

made me realize that everyone is different, and if your emotional makeup is different, it's hard to communicate. It's insulting, but more sad and pitiful to befoul true love. I reject all negative attitudes to love. In the Bible there's a story of Amnon and Tamar. Amnon was mad about his half-sister Tamar, and he raped her. Then he threw her out and locked the door behind her. I don't understand such behaviour. It all seems like part of the mystery of the human heart we can't understand. Just as we can't look inside Hamlet's heart.

Richard I suppose even sworn lovers could change. I'm not a psychiatrist, so I can't diagnose this state of Amnon's mind, but it appears to me like some mental illness or weakness. Dare I ask you this question? Can you tell me the real reason why you broke up with Hamlet?

Ophelia It all started because my father demanded that I obey him. He set up a scene so that the king could eavesdrop on our conversation. My father used me to entrap Hamlet, but Hamlet was too clever for that.

빠질 리가 없지요. 저만 배신자가 된 꼴로, 자존심 상하고 부끄럽고 수치스럽기 짝이 없었습니다.

리처드 하기 힘든 얘기를 그리 들려주니, 고맙소.

오필리아 다 지나간 옛날 얘긴 걸요. 이건 다른 얘기인데요, 군주님. 아니, 리처드, 런던서 활동하는 벨몬트의 포샤를 아시지요?

리처드 런던 금융계의 여왕, 벨몬트 재단의 포샤를 모르는 사람이 이 나라에 있겠소?

오필리아 포샤가 오는 추수 감사절에 맞춰서 자선 가면무도회를 계획하고 있어요. 제가 그 행사를 돕고 있는데, 가면무도회에 군주님을 초대해도 될까요?

리처드 정말 가슴 떨리는 초대요. 고맙기 그지없지만, 가면무도회라면 나 같은 사람과는 어울리지 않소. 나의 뒤틀린 절뚝발이 형체가 무슨 수로 가려지겠소? 어떤 가면이 이 몸을 숨겨 줄 수 있겠소? 더군다나 난 춤출 줄도 모른다오. 그래서 파티에 가본 기억이 거의 없소. 어쩔 수 없이 참석해야 했을 때는 한두 바퀴 도는 시늉만 하고 살짝 빠져나온 기억만 있을 뿐이오.

오필리아 저도 춤추는 건 좋아하지 않아요.

리처드 엘시노 궁에서 무도회가 많이 열렸을 텐데.

오필리아 그 시절에는 그랬어요. 지금은 관심이 없는데, 그래도 포샤

He thought I betrayed him. I was so embarrassed, ashamed and humiliated.

Richard Thank you for telling me your painful experience.

Ophelia Well, it's all over now. This is a different topic, Your Majesty, I mean Richard, but do you know Portia of Belmont, who now lives in London?

Richard The queen of the financial world! Who in this country hasn't heard of Portia and her Belmont Foundation?

Ophelia Portia is planning a masquerade ball for Thanksgiving charity and I'm helping her organize it. Can I invite you?

Richard That's too kind of you! The thought of going makes my heart beat. But in truth I'm not fit for a masquerade. How can I disguise my limp, and what costume will conceal my deformed body? Also, I can't dance. I don't ever remember going to a party, and on occasions when I had to make an appearance, I left immediately.

Ophelia I don't like dancing either.

Richard But there must have been hundreds of balls at Elsinore.

Ophelia Oh, yes, there were then. I have no interest in balls

의 가면무도회는 자선 무도회라서 마음이 끌려요. 군주님께 함께 가주십사고 하면 너무 무리한 요청일까요? 포샤한테 리처드 군주님이 함께 참석한다고 하면, 대환영일 텐데요.

리처드 그건 그대의 착각이오. 내가 악명 높은 리처드 3세인 줄 알면 손님들이 도망할지도 모르오. 다행히 가면에 가려서 나를 알아볼 자는 없겠지만.

오필리아 제가 군주님인 줄 알고 도망가던가요? 그거야말로 군주님의 착각이십니다.

리처드 런던 시내에 절름발이가 나 하나는 아닐 터이니, 그렇다면, 한번 시도해 볼까요? 아무래도 내가 님프에게 홀린 것 같소. 바사니오 녀석이 장가 하나는 끝내주게 잘 갔구려. 그자의 혈통은 귀족이라지만 타고난 건달이지 않습니까.

오필리아 그건 과거지사고요. 지금은 포샤와 함께 벨몬트 재단을 위해 열심히 일하고 있어요. 그라쉬아노, 로렌조 등을 비롯한 바사니오 친구들이 모두 포샤 회사에 근무하고 있답니다.

리처드 베니스의 가출자들이 가면무도회에 무더기로 출몰하겠군.

오필리아 가출자요? 재미난 표현을 쓰시네요.

리처드 제시카는 아버지 샤일록을 증오하고 못 견디겠다고 남자로 변장해서 남친 로렌조와 함께 야반도주했잖소. 아버지 샤일록의 금괴를 훔쳐 달아난 그 불량소녀가 제시카 아니오?

now, but Portia's masquerade is a charity ball, and that's why I'm helping. Would it be too much of an imposition to ask you to come? Portia would be delighted to have you.

Richard You're mistaken there. If they knew that I'm the infamous Richard III, they would all run away. A mask might help, though I doubt it.

Ophelia Did I run away when I saw you approach? You're the one who's mistaken.

Richard Well, I suppose I can't be the only person in London with a limp. Shall I venture? You must have bewitched me to make me say that. I must say Bassanio made a really good marriage. He comes from a good family, but is in truth a useless loafer.

Ophelia That was in the past. He's now working hard with Portia for the Foundation. In fact, Gratiano, Lorenzo and other friends of his are all working there.

Richard A union of the home-leavers of Venice, I see.

Ophelia "Home-leavers"? What do you mean?

Richard Well, didn't Jessica disguise herself as a man and elope with her boyfriend Lorenzo in the middle of the night? All because she hated her father Shylock. She stole her father's chest of gold like a thief, and

아버지가 애지중지 아끼는 죽은 아내의 가락지를 원숭이와 바꿔버린, 철딱서니 없는 계집아이 말이오.

오필리아 그래도 벨몬트의 달밤 아래 로렌조와 제시카가 서로 주고받는 연시는 듣는 이의 가슴을 포근히 적셔주지 않습니까?

리처드 머리는 가볍고 가슴만 뜨거우면 그런 구절이 절로 나오는 모양이오.

오필리아 군주님은 머리와 가슴을 갈라치시네요.

리처드 영특하신 오필리아 아가씨, 새겨듣겠소이다. 어쨌든 바사니오는 탕아였소. 향락 생활에 가진 돈을 몽땅 탕진한 그가 갑부 상속녀 포샤의 재산을 노린 거 아니오? 타락한 상업 도시에서 평생 농땡이로 살 줄 알았던 그자가 그래도 일을 한다니, 듣던 중 반가운 소식이오. 하나님은 일하기 싫으면 먹지도 말라 하셨소. 포샤는 진정한 계몽가로군. 놀랍소. 그것도 그 여인의 능력이니, 셰익스피어 어른이 아주 좋아하겠구려.

오필리아 규칙적인 생활에 익숙지 않던 사람들이지만 그래도 열심히 일하는 모습이 대견해요.

리처드 포샤는 법률과 재무에 탁월한 여인이오. 포샤 없는 베니스의 위장이 홀쭉해지지는 않았나 모르겠소. 허허.

오필리아 군주님은 말씀을 재밌게 하십니다.

exchanged her mother's ring that he cherished for a monkey! She was a naughty thoughtless girl!

Ophelia But it warms your heart to listen to their lovers' talk under the moon in Belmont.

Richard I suppose such words are possible if your heart is warm, even if the head is light and empty.

Ophelia You're splitting up the head and the heart, and you shouldn't.

Richard My sagacious Ophelia, I'll bear that in mind. But Bassanio was an idler. He wasted his fortune and wanted to marry Portia for her money. But I'm glad to hear that he's working. I thought he would spend his entire life idling in that corrupt commercial city. God told you not to eat if you don't work. Portia is a true enlightened being. Shakespeare would have liked her a lot.

Ophelia Bassanio is not used to regular routines, but it's good to see him working hard.

Richard Portia's knowledge of the law and finance is outstanding. Venice's treasury must have become poorer for her leaving it.

Ophelia That's an amusing way of seeing it.

리처드 그런데 말이오. 미안하오만, 난 포샤와 바사니오의 사랑을 회의적으로 봅니다. 바사니오가 포샤에게 날아든 동기는 오로지 재력이 탐난 것이었소. 본인 입으로 그렇게 밝혔소. 포샤도 그래요. 상대가 어떤 인품인지 대화도 한번 나누어 보지 않고, 서로 간에 서로를 발견하는 시간 없이, 그렇게 사모했다는 게 나로선 이해가 잘 안되오. 하기는 그 당시 연애사라는 게 모두 그 수준이었으니까. 그저 외모만 보고 반하는 건데, 그럴 수도 있을 거요. 그러다 보니 예쁘게 보이려고 얼굴에 덕지덕지 처발라대는 여인들의 행태를 본 햄릿이 이를 역겨워하고 비난했지요. 지금 이 시대는 화장술이 문제가 아니라오. 아예 입맛대로 얼굴을 뜯어고치는 성형술이 발달했으니까. 처녀 때 고친 얼굴이 임종 때 허물어지면, 이를 알아보지 못한 남편이, "오, 이 얼굴이 내가 보고 즐기던 그 얼굴이냐?" 흡사 파우스트 박사의 대사를 모방할 것 같지 않소? 허허!

오필리아 군주님은 배우 같으셔요. 정말 재밌는 분이시네요. 교회 구석에 조용히 앉아계실 때의 모습과는 전혀 딴판이시네요.

리처드 오필리아 아가씨! 나는 그대를 지켜보았소. 그대의 혈통이 양반 태생인 줄은 알고 있소만, 내가 그대를 진정한 귀족으로 간주하는 것은 혈통 때문이 아니오. 그대의 온전한

Richard I'm sorry to disagree with you about Portia and Bassanio. I don't look upon their love as genuine. Bassanio sought Portia only for her fortune, and Portia said she loved him, but they didn't exchange many words before they got married. They had no time to get to know each other. So I don't understand their love. Well, I suppose that kind of marriage was normal in those days. They just go for appearance. Hamlet saw through it all, and found women who lard themselves with makeup nauseating. But nowadays, it's not the question of makeup, I'm told. I understand that plastic surgery is the latest thing, and women have this and that done to their faces to improve their looks. When a husband sees the face of his wife on her deathbed and doesn't recognize her any longer because all the changes she had made in her youth have become undone, he could well say after Faustus, "Is this the face that I loved?"

Ophelia You're very amusing. You'd make a good actor.

Richard I've observed you for a while, and I know that you're of noble blood. But the reason I regard you as a true aristocrat is not on that account. I see it

인간미에서 찾은 거요. 고백할진대, 그대의 그 미덕에 내가 심히 흔들린 것이오.

오필리아 군주님의 말씀에 제가 몸 둘 바를 모르겠네요. 외모만 보고도 한눈에 반할 수 있다는 현상을 저는 충분히 이해하거든요. 군주님과 헤어지기 서운하지만 이제 그만 일어나야 할 시간이 되었네요. 이렇게 군주님을 뵐 수 있으니, 공원에 오기를 참 잘했어요. 일요일에는 교회에서 뵙고 인사드려도 괜찮겠지요? 예배 끝나기 전에 자리를 뜨지 마시고, 그대로 계시면 제가 찾아뵙겠습니다. 저는 찬양대에 있거든요.

리처드 아, 꾀꼬리 님프시라! 알겠소. 내 고정 자리에 망부석처럼 박혀 있으리다.

오필리아 무지개가 아직도 흐릿하게 보이네요. 그럼 안녕, 군주님! 리처드! (*오필리아는 퇴장한다.*)

리처드 (*혼잣말로*) 오, 이게 꿈이냐, 생시냐? 내가 오필리아와 일요일마다 만난다고? 그녀와 무도회에 간다고? 맥베스 형님께 내가 오필리아와 진도 나갈 일 없다고 큰소리쳤는데. 형님! 그건 내 본심이, 내 진심이 아니었소. 오필리아의 유령을 안고 자는 게 아니라, 실체를 안고 잠자리에 들 날이 머지않은 것 같소. "꿈은 이루어진다!" 랄랄라! (페이드아웃.)

in your unsullied integrity. To confess, it was your virtue that moved me.

Ophelia I'm embarrassed by the compliments you pay me. But I understand people falling for looks. I'm sorry to leave you, but it's time for me to go. I'm glad I came to the park, as it was a pleasure to talk to you. Can I say hello when we meet in church? Don't go away before the service is over, and I'll come over. I'm in the choir.

Richard Ah! a lark? All right, I'll stay put in my place.

Ophelia I can still see the rainbow, though it's fading. Good-bye, Your Majesty, I mean Richard! (*Ophelia leaves.*)

Richard (*To himself*) Am I dreaming or what? Meet Ophelia every Sunday! Go to a ball with her! I assured Macbeth I had no intention of winning her, but I can't have meant it. The day when I'll be sleeping with her in my arms rather than with her ghost is not far off. Dreams can come true, tra la la. . . . (Fade out.)

[장면 4] 에필로그 계속. 리처드 3세와 맥베스의 대화.

(페이드인. *리처드가 눈을 감고 벤치에 기대어 잠들어 있다. 그를 발견한 맥베스는 매우 놀라면서 흔들어 깨운다.*)

맥베스 여보게, 리처드! 이게 어떻게 된 거냐? 아니, 여기서 잠자고 있다니! 아이고, 망측해라! 입가에 미소 띤 걸 보니 단꿈까지 꾼 모양일세. 아무 때고, 아무 데서나 잠잘 수 있는 자네의 심신이 부럽기는 하네만. 그렇지만 이건 아니지! 이건 참말 아니네! (*심하게 그를 흔들면서*) 여보게, 리처드 3세여! 체면 좀 지키시게! 군주가 공원에서 낮잠을 자다니! 세상에 이런 일이 다 있냐!

리처드 형님은 왜 아직도 안 가고 여기 계신 거요?

맥베스 난리 치는 백조들 구경하고 있었네. 리처드 글로스터! 대체 어떻게 된 일인가? 붕어들 밥 줘야 한다고 서두를 때는 언제고, 예서 잠을 자고 있으니, 이게 무슨 망측한 일이냐?

[Scene 4] Epilogue continued.
Richard III and Macbeth talking.

(Fade in. *Richard is asleep on a bench. Macbeth is surprised to find him there and wakes him.*)

Macbeth Richard, my boy, Richard, what are you doing here. You've been fast asleep, and it's unseemly, I tell you. You were smiling in your sleep too, so you must have been dreaming of something nice. I so envy your ability to sleep anywhere. But this won't do. (*Shaking him violently*) Richard, Richard III, think of your position, a king to fall asleep in the park like a vagabond! Who has ever seen such a sight!

Richard Oh, are you still here? I thought you had left.

Macbeth I was watching the swans. Richard of Gloucester, what's the matter with you? I thought you had to hurry away to feed your fish. But to find you

자네 혹시 불치의 졸음 병에라도 걸린 건 아닌가?

리처드 내가 여기서 잤다고? 이 벤치에서? 형님, 여기 오는 길에, 혹시 오필리아를 보지 못하였소?

맥베스 오필리아라니! 무슨 잠꼬대야? 이거, 큰일 났군!

리처드 봄날의 헛꿈이라고? 내 머리에 당나귀 대가리라도 붙었소?

맥베스 당나귀 대가리는 또 뭐냐? 티타니아 품에서 꿀잠이라도 잤다는 게냐? 리처드 3세가 공원에서 잠을 자다니! 이게 무슨 해괴한 일이냐? 어서 정신 차리시게! 이러다 병나면 큰일 나겠다! 자네 계획대로면, 동방에 가서 할매 교수도 만나야 할 것 아닌가?

리처드 지당하신 말씀이오! 악인 이미지를 씻어 줄 나의 구원의 할매 교수를, 그 괴짜 여인을 꼬옥 만나야 하고말고! 그런데ㅡ 내가 여기서 낮잠을 잤다는 거요?

맥베스 여보게, 늘어지게 잔 모양일세.

리처드 그게 꿈이었다고? 백일몽? 삼베 바지에 방귀 빠지듯 사라진 헛꿈이라고? 이 벤치에 나란히 앉아서 내가 오필리아와 단둘이 나눈 대화가 그럼 모두 일장춘몽이었단 말이오?

맥베스 내가 자네 꿈을 어찌 알겠나? 꿈속에 나도 있던가?

sleeping here. Have you caught sleeping sickness or something?

Richard I slept? on this bench? Macbeth, have you seen Ophelia on your way here?

Macbeth Ophelia? What Ophelia? You're dreaming! Oh my God, what are you up to?

Richard A midspring day's dream? Do I have an ass's head on mine?

Macbeth An ass's head? What nonsense is all this? I suppose you were having sweet dreams in Titania's arms, eh? To see a king sleeping in the park! What indignity! Get up, get up or you'll catch something, sleeping in the open like this. I thought you had to go and meet some old lady professor.

Richard You're right. She'll be my saviour who will wash me clean of my infamous image. I must meet that eccentric old lady. But . . . did I really take a nap here?

Macbeth Yes, and soundly too.

Richard So that was a dream, a day dream! A vain dream that just vanished like smoke! I was talking with Ophelia on this bench, and all that was a mere dream? I can't believe it.

Macbeth How can I tell what you dreamed? Was I in your dream too?

리처드 "믿음은 바라는 것의 실상"이라고 했는데. 내 꿈은 내가 바라는 것의 실상이 아닌가? 허상인가? 형님, "현실이냐, 환상이냐? 실제냐, 환각이냐?" 이거 셰익스피어가 주로 다룬 주제 아니오? 그러니까, 형님이 오필리아를 보지 못했다, 그 말이오? 그럼, 무지개는 보았소?

맥베스 난데없이 무지개는 왜 찾아? 이 사람 완전히 넋이 나갔군! 꿈에 오필리아가 무지개 타고 오더냐? 리처드 글로스터! 정신 차리고, 어서 일어나시게! 꿈 깨고, 그만 일어나라고! 짝사랑엔 약도 없다는데, 큰일 났다.

리처드 약이 없기는 왜 없소! 사랑의 묘약, 하늘의 계시라는 게 있소이다.

맥베스 에구, 자네가 다니엘이냐? 지금 자네가 계시 운운할 때가 아닐세.

리처드 형님은 내가 목을 매고 사랑할 여자가 생겼으면 하고 바라지 않았소? 제이퀴즈가 오드리와 터치스톤을 맺어준 그런 역할을 형님도 내게 해주고 싶다 하지 않았소? 내가 그 금쪽같은 기회를 형님께 드리리다. 이번 주일에 형님과 나, 우리 둘이서 함께 교회 가는 거요.

맥베스 아이고, 이제 교회까지 끌어들이는가? 갈수록 태산일세.

리처드 교회에서 판정이 날 것이오.

Richard The Bible says, "Now faith is the substance of things hoped for, the evidence of things not seen". So is my dream the substance of things I hope for? Or is it mere illusion, Macbeth? Is it reality or fantasy? What is real and what illusory? Isn't this what Shakespeare is all about? So you didn't see Ophelia? But did you see the rainbow?

Macbeth What rainbow? You're talking nonsense. Did Ophelia come to you in your dream riding on a rainbow? Richard dear, Richard, Gloucester, wake up and come back to reality, please get up. Oh my God, we're in trouble now. There's no antidote to unrequited love.

Richard No cure? But there's a thing called the elixir of love, and also revelations from heaven.

Macbeth So you think you are Daniel now, eh? This is no time to be talking of revelations.

Richard You wanted me to give my life for love, didn't you? Didn't you want to play the role that Jacques played for Audrey and Touchstone? I'll give you that precious opportunity. This Sunday you and I are going to church.

Macbeth Church? Why bring church into all this? I'm completely at sea.

Richard The verdict will be given in church.

맥베스 교회가 짝짓기 재판소냐?

리처드 내 경우는 그렇소. 그리고, 형님! 올가을 추수 감사절 때는 벨몬트 재단의 자선 가면무도회에 우리가 참석합니다. 거기서 형님도 조신하고 올곧은 코딜리아 같은 귀부인을 만날지 누가 압니까? 이제 형님은 '사랑의 불모지', 그 명예롭지 못한 갑옷을 벗는 거요. 이 리처드 글로스터도 자존심이라는 굴레를 끊겠소. 하긴, 나 같은 자가 무슨 자존심 따질 군번이나 되는가요! 알고 보면, '사랑'이란 두 글자에 나는 매우 심약한 남자요. 형님, 이제부터 우리의 황무지를 푸른 초장과 옥토로 일굽시다.

맥베스 혼자서 북 치고, 장구 치고, 잘하시네! 춤도 추지 그러는가?

리처드 암요! 춰야지요. 셰익스피어와 함께 춤을! 아― 형님! 우리 댄스 학원에 등록합시다. 가면무도회에서 오필리아와 춤을 추려면 그 아가씨 발등 밟는 실수는 범하지 않아야 할 것 아니오? 우리 빙글빙글 돌아보자고요.

맥베스 아이고, 자네가 도는 게 아니라, 내가 돌아 버리겠다! 이보게, 대체 어찌 된 노릇이냐? 자네가 획 가버렸어!

리처드 예, 형님! 우리 함께 획 가버립시다. 활짝 웃는 희극 세계로! 셰익스피어의 <좋으실 대로>처럼 우리도 결혼의 신, 하이멘

Macbeth What verdict? Surely you don't regard the church as a kind of matchmaking court?

Richard In my case, I do. Also, Macbeth, let's go together to the Thanksgiving ball given by the Belmont Foundation. Who knows whether you won't meet an honest and pure lady like Cordelia. You must throw off the stigma of being an emotional desert, and I, Richard, will cut the bondage of my pride. In fact, it's laughable that such a one as I should even talk of pride. To tell the truth, I am a weak man before the word "love". Let's turn the desert and wilderness into green and fertile fields, Macbeth.

Macbeth You do that all on your own. The show is all yours, my boy. You might sing and dance as well.

Richard And why not? I will dance with Shakespeare. Let's enroll ourselves on dance classes. If I were to dance with Ophelia, I must learn at least not to step on her toes. Let's whirl about.

Macbeth You go and do that, and I tell you, my head is already whirling. What's the matter with you? What madness is this?

Richard Yes, Macbeth, let's both be mad, you and I. And rush to the world of comedy, our faces bright with smiles. Don't you think we too deserve to stand before

앞에 서야 하지 않겠소? 그 희극에서 몇 쌍이나 짝이 맺어지는지 형님 기억하시오?

맥베스 (*퉁명스럽게*) 몰라. 난 기억 없네!

리처드 물경 일곱 쌍이나 합동 결혼을 합니다. 코리아의 할매 교수가 우리도 하이멘 앞에 세워서, 합동 혼례 장면을 멋지게 보여 주기를 기대하오.

맥베스 극은 아무나 쓰냐더니! 혼자서 잘도 꾸며대는구나!

리처드 셰익스피어 어른이시여, 서운해 하지 마오. 맥베스 형님과 나는 우리의 운명의 쳇바퀴를 한번 돌려볼 생각이라오. 그래서 런던시 행복동으로 이사하렵니다.

맥베스 리처드 글로스터! 자네나 이사를 하든지 말든지! 난 소중한 나의 독백을 지킬 것이네. 정신 차리게, 이 사람아! 헛꿈 꿨다더니, 헛소리만 계속 늘어놓는구나. 큰 병 나기 전에, 자네 아무래도 이쯤에서 셰익스피어 그림자를 벗어나야겠다.

리처드 모르시는 말씀! 형님이나 나나 셰익스피어의 그림자를 벗어나면 우린 빈껍데기요. 존재 없는 제로요, 제로! 덧셈도 뺄셈도 안 되는, 아무것도 아닌, 절대 제로! 그걸 모르시오?

맥베스 그럼 변하지 않는 불변의 존재로군.

Hymen as in *As You Like It*? Do you remember how many couples were born in that play?

Macbeth (*Rather crossly*) I have no idea, and I don't care.

Richard As many as seven couples. I'm looking forward to the day when that old lady professor from Korea will make us stand before Hymen and give us a grand wedding.

Macbeth You said not everyone is a writer, but you seem to be apt at making things up.

Richard Gentle Shakespeare, don't be offended. Macbeth and I are about to turn the wheel of fortune and move to Happy Street in London.

Macbeth You, Richard of Gloucester, you move to Happy Street in London. I'm going to guard my precious soliloquy. Stop all this nonsense and get up. Your nonsensical dream is making you jabber. You need to free yourself from Shakespeare's shadow before things get too serious.

Richard No, no, it's you who don't understand. If we free ourselves from Shakespeare's shadow, we're nothing but empty shells, a zero with no substance, a mere zero that you can neither add nor subtract, absolute nothing. Don't you know that?

Macbeth Then we will never change and remain eternally the same.

리처드 존재가 없는데 불변할 게 뭐가 있단 말이오? 형님의 그 소중한 독백은 이 세상 끝날 때까지 누가 뺏어가지 않을 것이니, 맘 푹 놓으시고. 크리스토퍼 말로 맥베스를 탄생시켜 줄 제2의 맥베스 부인 꿈이나 꾸시오.

맥베스 헛소리 그만하고 어서 일어나라니까!

리처드 형님이 극찬하는 임윤찬 연주나, 캘리밴 독백보다 더 빛나는 주옥같은 사랑의 독백이, 대시인 맥베스 입에서 터져 나올지 누가 압니까? 로렌조와 제시카 같은 얼치기 애들도 연애 시를 줄줄이 읊어대는 판에 말이오.

맥베스 이보게, 제발 그만 일어나시게! 언제는 오필리아와 진도 나갈 일 없다더니, 어이 딴청인가?

리처드 난 일편단심이오. 일편단심!

맥베스 심약한 순정파가 아니라더니! 자네는 확실히 청개구리 맞다.

리처드 오, 약한 자여, 그대의 이름은— 남자니라!

맥베스 자, 일어납시다! 미스터 일편단심! 청개구리! 어서 일어나라니까!

리처드 (*비틀거리고 일어나면서 찬송가 가락을 읊는다.*) 세상 풍조는 나날이 변하여도 나는 내 믿음 지키리니!— (*맥베스는 리처드를 부축하고, 두 사람은 퇴장한다.* 페이드아웃.)

Richard What do you mean eternally the same? How can something that doesn't exist be eternal? Dear Macbeth, no one will take your precious soliloquy away from you. It will be yours until doomsday, so don't worry about it, and go and dream of the second Lady Macbeth who will give you Christopher Marlowe Macbeth.

Macbeth Stop talking nonsense and get up, I beg of you.

Richard Who knows you may not utter one day a beautiful soliloquy on love that will surpass Yunchan Lim's performance or Caliban's speech? Even idiots like Lorenzo and Jessica can spout love poems at will, so what will prevent you?

Macbeth Please get up now. You swore you're not interested in Ophelia, but just look at you now.

Richard I'm completely devoted to her, but completely.

Macbeth And you say you're not romantic? You sure are a riddle.

Richard "Oh frailty, thy name is man."

Macbeth All right, let's get up now, Mr. Devotion! Get up I say.

Richard (*Gets up shakily, humming a hymn.*) "It will still be my stay when the fashions of earth in the mist are dissolving away." (*Both leave the stage, Macbeth supporting Richard.* Fade out.)

저자 송옥

고려대학교 명예 교수로, 고려대학교에서 학사 학위, 센트럴 워싱턴 대학교에서 석사 학위, 오리건 대학교에서 박사 학위를 받고, 고려대학교에서 영문학과 극문학을 가르쳤다.
Oak Song, professor emeritus at Korea University, received her BA from Korea University, Master's from Central Washington University and Ph.D from University of Oregon, and taught English and Dramatic Literature at Korea University.

역자 문희경

고려대학교 명예 교수로, 옥스퍼드 대학교에서 학사, 석사, 박사 학위를 받고, 고려대학교에서 영문학을 가르쳤다.
Hi Kyung Moon, professor emeritus at Korea University, received her BA and M.Phil. and D. of Phil. from Oxford University and taught English Literature at Korea University.

셰익스피어의 그림자 Shakespeare's Shadow

초판 1쇄 발행일 2024년 4월 3일

송 옥 지음
문희경 옮김

발 행 인 이성모
발 행 처 도서출판 동인 / 서울특별시 종로구 혜화로3길 5, 118호
등록번호 제1-1599호
대표전화 (02) 765-7145 / FAX (02) 765-7165
홈페이지 www.donginbook.co.kr
이 메 일 donginpub@naver.com
I S B N 978-89-5506-964-8 (03840)
정 가 13,000원